Symphony of Screams

A Horror Novel By Kit Lewis

Copyright © 2024 by Kit Lewis All rights reserved.

The content contained within this book may not be reproduced, duplicated, or transmitted without direct written permission from the author or the publisher.

Under no circumstances will any blame or legal responsibility be held against the publisher, or author, for any damages, reparation, or monetary loss due to the information contained within this book, either directly or indirectly.

Legal Notice:

This book is copyright-protected. It is only for personal use. You cannot amend, distribute, sell, use, quote, or paraphrase any part, or the content within this book, without the consent of the author or publisher.

Disclaimer Notice:

Please note the information contained within this document is for educational and entertainment purposes only. All efforts have been executed to present accurate, up-to-date, reliable, and complete information. No warranties of any kind are declared or implied. Readers acknowledge that the author is not engaged in the rendering of legal, financial, medical, or professional advice. The content within this book has been derived from various sources.

Please consult a licensed professional before attempting any techniques outlined in this book.

By reading this document, the reader agrees that under no circumstances is the author responsible for any losses, direct or indirect, that are incurred as a result of the use of the information contained within this document, including, but not limited to, errors, omissions, or inaccuracies.

No portion of this book may be reproduced in any form without written permission from the publisher or author, except as permitted by U.S. copyright law.

SYMPHONY OF SCREAMS

This is a work of fiction. Names, characters, places, and incidents are from the author's imagination or used fictitiously. Any resemblance to people or places is coincidental.

Contents

1. Weekly Occurrence — 1
2. Cries For Help — 15
3. Dr. Blackwell — 24
4. The Plan — 29
5. Mothers Revenge — 35
6. Sarah's Happy Place — 48
7. The Game of Life — 55
8. Hard Decision — 69
9. The Caring Doctor — 80
10. The Student — 86
11. Fixing Dad — 95
12. Great Escape — 98
13. Finishing The Game — 104
14. Will It Ever End — 111
15. No Escape — 124

16. Returning Home   131

17. My Fate Now Sealed   139

18. Join my newsletter   145

Weekly Occurrence

In the languid grip of dusk, the small, remote town of Talmage wore its silence like a cloak, untouched by the winds of change that had swept through much of America in the late 1960s. Nestled between the gnarled woods and the restless rolling hills, it was a place where time seemed to trickle slowly, like the blood of history seeping through the cracks of its forgotten pathways.

On a particularly dim evening in October, under the sigh of the dying light, I sat on the worn wooden steps of my family's farmhouse, lost in the pages of a book. The fading sun threw shadows that danced silently across the text, blurring the lines between the horrors within the pages and the tranquility of my surroundings. At twenty, my eyes were too curious for this small town, and my heart too restless for its pace.

As dusk deepened, casting a gloomy shroud over the landscape, the sudden, piercing scream of terror sliced through the quiet evening like a knife. My heart hammered violently against my chest, jolted by the intensity of the cry. Peering through the thickening mist, I glimpsed a figure stumbling frantically down the road leading away from the foreboding River Road Asylum—a place so often spoken of in hushed tones in town, it might as well have been a character from one of my dark, twisted tales.

The man's movements were erratic, fueled by sheer panic, as if he were desperately fleeing some unseen horror nipping at his heels. His terror-filled screams echoed into the twilight, a simple soundtrack to his desperate flight, conveying a primal fear so palpable it chilled the very air.

As I strained to see more through the encroaching darkness, his form became a blur, and then, just as quickly as the horrifying tableau had appeared, it vanished. The night reclaimed its stillness, swallowing up the man and his cries, leaving behind a haunting silence that hung heavily around me, thick with unanswered questions and the echo of dread.

As I sat on the worn wooden steps of my family's farmhouse, the unsettling image of a man in white and his hapless burden replayed in my mind. The twilight world of the book I was reading had breached the boundary into reality, the lines between fiction and life blurring unsettlingly. I couldn't shake the vividness of what I'd seen; the bleak contrast of blood against the man's white shirt, the silent, efficient movements of his captor, and their ghostly disappearance back into the mist.

In the days that followed, an eerie sense of unease settled over Talmage. The quiet town, usually a sanctuary from the chaos of the outside world, seemed to be holding its breath, bracing for something unknown. As I went about my daily routines, my eyes were inexorably drawn back to the road leading to River Road Asylum. Each time, something odd would catch my attention—a fleeting shadow behind the wrought-iron gates, distant cries that were cut short, as if muffled by the thick, ancient walls.

The incidents grew more frequent and more disturbing. One evening, as the sun dipped below the horizon, painting the sky in bruised purples and reds, I saw a small group of figures gathered at the edge of the woods near the asylum. They were huddled together, and all I could hear was their whispers carried through the cool afternoon breeze. It was unclear whether they were planning an escape or some covert meeting, but the secrecy of their gathering was palpable even from a distance.

Another morning brought the sight of an ambulance speeding down the gravel path that wound its way up to the asylum's main entrance. The siren was silent, its lights a cold, intermittent flash in the foggy dawn. The vehicle didn't return, and no explanation filtered down to the townspeople, leaving a residue of speculative theories in its wake.

These mysterious occurrences compounded the atmosphere of dread that seemed to cling to the asylum like the ivy on its old stone walls. Each day, as I watched from a distance, the line between observer and participant thinned. My curiosity, coupled with a growing sense of responsibility to understand what was happening, compelled me to keep vigil. I found myself taking long walks that invariably ended at the boundaries of the asylum's grounds, my gaze scouring the landscape for any clue that might explain the strange events.

The townsfolk, normally a tight-knit community, began to show signs of strain. Conversations would halt as I approached, eyes darting away, voices dropping to whispers. It was clear that fear, and perhaps some dark knowledge, was seeping into everyone's thoughts. What little I could glean from overheard snippets and reluctant exchanges suggested a collective awareness of something amiss at the asylum, but no one was willing to discuss it openly.

As time went on, my fascination turned into an obsession. The need to uncover the truth behind the eerie happenings at the asylum consumed me, pushing me to take more risks, to get closer to the heart of the mystery. What had started as a distant, almost detached observation had morphed into a personal crusade, one that drew me ever deeper into the shadows cast by the towering spires of River Road Asylum.

Every afternoon, as the sun began its slow descent behind the rolling hills that cradled Talmage, I positioned an old wooden chair at the edge of our front yard. From here, the road leading to the old asylum stretched out before me like a ribbon through the fields, its secrets veiled in the distance. With a notepad and pencil, I settled into a routine of watchfulness, the pages gradually filling with notes and sketches, a tangible record of the shadowy occurrences that intrigued and unnerved me.

The chair, weathered from years of exposure, creaked under my weight, adding a rhythmic accompaniment to the rustling of the leaves and the distant, haunting sounds that emanated from the direction of the asylum. The air around me was thick with the scent of late autumn—damp earth and decaying leaves—a pungent reminder of the cycle of death and rebirth in nature. This backdrop set a somber stage for my observations as if nature itself was in tune with the darker undercurrents flowing from the old institution.

My notepad became a catalog of abnormalities. One entry detailed the erratic behavior of Turkey Vultures near the asylum; they seemed to swarm the area in a frenzied cluster before dispersing abruptly as if repelled by some unseen force. Another note described the way the mist seemed to cling more stubbornly to the asylum grounds than anywhere else in town, swirling in patterns that almost looked like whispering ghosts.

As the days grew shorter and the nights longer, the air chilled, wrapping the town in a cold embrace that seemed to mirror the growing dread within me. One particularly evening, as the sun dipped below the horizon and twilight took its claim, I witnessed a sudden burst of activity at the asylum. Several figures emerged hurriedly from a side door, their bodies bent against a burgeoning wind, carrying between them what looked distressingly like a body wrapped in sheets. They moved with a hurried, desperate pace, disappearing into an awaiting van that drove off with such speed it kicked up a cloud of dust that hung in the air like a shroud.

Sketching these scenes, I tried to capture not just the actions but the atmosphere—the palpable aura of fear and secrecy that seemed to emanate from the asylum like a dark energy. My hand trembled slightly as I drew, not just from the cold but from the adrenal surge that came with witnessing these clandestine activities.

At night, the sounds from the asylum grew more pronounced. Cries, sometimes distant, sometimes alarmingly close, drifted across the fields. On windless nights, these lamentations carried with an eerie clarity, stirring unease that prickled at the back of my neck. Scribbling down these auditory encounters, I noted the times, the intensity, and my speculative thoughts on their origins.

These solitary vigils became my obsession, each day's watch adding layers to the unsettling tapestry of the asylum's hidden life. My notebook was no longer just a collection of observations; it was a dossier of potential evidence, hinting at unspeakable practices shrouded behind the asylum's stately facade.

Yet, with each passing day, as I sat in my creaking wooden chair and watched the shadows grow longer, a part of me knew that mere observation from a distance was no longer sufficient. The truth was calling me, a siren song that promised answers yet threatened deeper horrors. The line between observer and investigator was blurring, and I felt an inevitable pull towards the heart of the mystery, towards the gates of River Road Asylum itself.

One particular scene began to repeat with unsettling regularity, etching itself into the fabric of my daily observations and deeply into my psyche. Each afternoon, as the sun painted the sky in hues of orange and purple, a man would burst forth from the tree line that bordered the road leading to the asylum. Clad in the unmistakable bleached white fabric of a patient's gown, which flapped wildly around his thin, frantic frame, he ran with a desperation that was palpable even from the distance of my front yard.

Close on his heels, almost shadow-like in their persistence, was a guard dressed in the depressing, official white uniform of the asylum. His face set in grim determination, he pursued the fleeing man with a hunter's focus, his steps thudding heavily on the hard-packed dirt of the road. The chase would unfold like a grim ballet, the two figures locked in a ghoulish dance that always ended the same way: the guard would tackle the patient just beyond the bend in the road, where the woods gave way to open fields. There, they would struggle briefly, disturbingly silent in their violent embrace, before the guard would drag the subdued patient back towards the asylum, disappearing from my view as they re-entered the tree line.

This recurring event became a darkly ritualistic part of my afternoons, each occurrence chipping away at any remaining notions I had of the asylum as a place of healing. The desperation of the fleeing man—the terror in his eyes, the heave of his breath, the barefoot pounding on the cold road—spoke of horrors faced within the asylum's walls that were bad enough to make him risk the almost certain pain of recapture and punishment.

Determined to understand more, I began to time my observations to coincide specifically with this event, my notepad filling with details not only of the chase but also of any nuances in the interaction that might tell me more about the patient, the guard, and the nature of their confinement. I noted the guard's efficiency and lack of hesitation, a professionalism that was as terrifying as it was impressive. It suggested a routine familiarity with such escapes as if they were an expected part of the asylum's daily rhythms.

One chilly evening, driven by a growing sense of responsibility and outrage, I decided to intervene. As the patient appeared, his gown whipping about his legs and his eyes wide with a wild fear, I stepped out from my observation post and onto the road. My presence startled him, causing a momentary pause in his flight—a pause that proved costly. The guard, seizing the opportunity, tackled him with renewed vigor, pinning him to the ground with a force that drove the air from my lungs in sympathetic pain.

"Go back inside!" the guard barked at me, his voice harsh and commanding. His eyes flicked to mine, a brief flash of recognition that I was the observer from the farmhouse.

Shaken, I retreated, the patient's whimpering cries echoing in my ears as I walked back to my chair. The reality of what I had witnessed—the raw, brutal struggle for freedom—solidified my resolve. I could no longer remain a passive observer. The repetitive nature of this event and the guard's reaction to my interference convinced me that what happened at the asylum was not just a series of isolated incidents but a systemic horror. I knew then that I needed to act, to delve deeper into the heart of the asylum's darkness, not just to witness but to expose and perhaps to help end the cycle of despair perpetuated behind its walls.

As the echo of their departure faded, I felt the chill of the October air seep into my bones. The asylum's silhouette loomed in the distance, its spires like the fingers of a gaunt hand scratching at the remnants of the light. I knew I should turn away, and retreat into the safety of my home, but the story was too compelling, the mystery too deep. The lines of my book blurred into the reality before me, and with a breath that felt like the first of my life, I followed the shadows into the night, drawn irresistibly toward the unfolding horror.

My steps were hesitant as I trailed behind the man in white, each footfall echoing my pounding heart. The dark path to the asylum was one I'd walked before, though never under such sinister circumstances.

The moon, a slender crescent, offered scant illumination, casting long, misshapen shadows that merged with the darkness enveloping the path.

As I neared the imposing iron gates of the asylum, I crouched behind the gnarled trunk of an old oak that had witnessed decades of sorrow spill from the stone walls it overshadowed. The air was thick with the scent of impending rain, mixing with the salt of the distant sea, a briny reminder of the vast, uncontrollable forces surrounding the town of Talmage.

The man in white approached the gates with a casual authority, his burden still slung over his shoulder, lifeless. At the gate, a guard emerged from a small, weather-beaten booth. The two men exchanged words that were lost in the wind, their voices a low murmur against the howling silence. With a reluctant nod, the guard swung open the heavy gates just enough to allow them passage before quickly securing them once more.

I watched, my breath forming clouds in the chill air, as the man in white disappeared through the asylum's large front doors, swallowed by the gaping maw of the building. The sight sent a shiver through me, a primal warning. The escapes from the asylum had become more frequent recently, each escapee appearing more terrified, more desperate not to return. Everyone was well aware of the horrors that happened in the asylum, but not many spoke of the mistreatment and madness, of a place forgotten by ethics and humanity.

It was no secret that River Road Asylum was on the brink of closure. Financial strains and a series of damning articles had left the institution teetering on the edge of scandal. Protests at its gates had escalated, and the townspeople were divided between fear of the inmates and... outrage over their conditions. I had heard it all at the local diner, seen the picket signs, and listened to the heated debates about the fate of those within the asylum's walls.

A rustling from the nearby brush snapped me back to the present. My heart leaped into my throat as I peered into the darkness, half-expecting to see another escapee or something worse. But it was just a fox, its eyes briefly catching the moonlight before it vanished into the undergrowth.

Realizing my vulnerability, I knew I should leave, that my curiosity had drawn me far enough into something that was rapidly spiraling beyond my control. Yet, as I turned to go, the soft, pitiful moan of someone in pain drifted from an open window above. It tugged at me, a silent plea in the night.

My decision was made in that instant. I couldn't walk away—not yet. I needed to know who was suffering, why they were suffering, and whether the rumors were true. With a deep breath, I slipped through the shadows along the perimeter wall, searching for another way in, driven by a mix of fear and determination. The night was deep, and within the walls of the asylum, it seemed even the darkness was alive with secrets waiting to be uncovered.

I crept closer to the source of the moans, my heart beating a frantic tattoo against my ribcage. The asylum's walls loomed above me, ancient and foreboding, pocked with small, barred windows that whispered tales of despair. I found the window from which the sounds had emanated—a grimy, cracked pane that offered a narrow view into the horrors within.

As I approached the window, urgency surged through me. The brick sill, just out of reach, seemed like my only portal to unseen terrors inside the asylum. My first attempt to grasp it was thwarted by the slick moss that clung to the bricks like a treacherous veneer, causing my fingers to slip helplessly away. Frustration welled within me as I scanned the surroundings for anything that might aid my ascent.

Nearby, a small plank of wood caught my eye, repurposed as an improvised border for the asylum's meticulously kept garden. Its position hinted at neglect, slightly askew from the others as if it had been less cared for. With a mixture of desperation and cautious optimism, I approached the plank, my movements hushed. Gripping its edges, I rocked it back and forth, feeling the resistance of the earth clasping it tight. With a final, determined tug, the plank gave way, releasing with a soft thud into the damp grass.

Heart pounding with the fear of being discovered, I moved as silently as possible, dragging the plank to the wall beneath the window. Positioning it carefully, I fashioned a makeshift ramp, the wood's surface rough and splintered under my hands. Stepping onto the lower end, I tested its stability before committing my full weight to it.

The plank groaned ominously under me but held firm, granting me those crucial extra inches needed to reach the window. With a deep breath, I hoisted myself up, my muscles straining against the pull of gravity. My hands, now gritty with the residue of moss and dirt, found a more secure grip on the sill. Pulling with all my might, I managed to elevate myself high enough to look through the window.

Peering through the dirt-streaked glass, my gaze adjusted to the dim light inside. The room was unadorned, the kind of bleakness that spoke of long, torturous hours with no respite. At first, all I could make out were shapes in various shades of gray, but as my eyes adapted, details began to emerge from the shadows.

Chained to a ring in the center of the floor was a man, his limbs splayed awkwardly as if he had collapsed from exhaustion or given up hope of escape. The chains clinked softly as he shifted, the sound eerily clear in the quiet night. The links were slick with blood, shining darkly under the faint light that filtered in from outside. It was obvious that the man had been struggling against his bonds, the skin around his wrists raw and torn.

As I watched, the man slowly turned his head, his movement labored, as if even that small act was a struggle against immense pain. Our eyes met, and I felt a chill ripple through me. The man's gaze was piercing, intense with a mix of madness and clarity that was unsettling. His mouth opened in a grotesque smile, revealing a dark, empty maw where teeth should have been, the gums oozing blood from jagged holes.

The sight was horrifying, yet there was something in the man's eyes that held me in place—a desperate plea for recognition, for humanity. Despite the gore, the smile seemed to be a tragic attempt at connection, a silent acknowledgment of another living soul witnessing his suffering.

I felt a surge of nausea and horror, mixed with a fierce, burning anger at the cruelty inflicted upon this man. My mind raced with questions—who was he? How had he ended up like this? What atrocities had been committed in the name of treatment or control within these walls?

Compelled by a need to do something—anything—to help, I looked around frantically for a way to enter the building. The window was too small, too high up to be of use. I needed to find a door, an unguarded entry that might allow me to reach the chained man.

With a last look at the prisoner, who still held my gaze, I lowered myself down and backed away from the window, my decision made. I would find a way in. I had to. The image of the man's bloody smile and the haunting desperation in his eyes would not let me turn away now.

Determined, I moved quickly along the wall, my tenacity hardening with every step. Tonight, the shadows of the asylum were deep and full of secrets, and I was about to dive headlong into their darkness.

Cries For Help

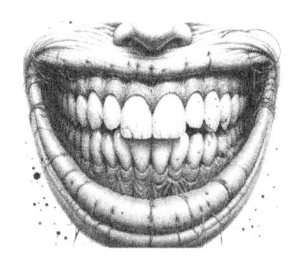

My heart pounded as I skirted the shadowed perimeter of River Road Asylum, my eyes scanning for any breach—an unlocked door, a loose window lattice, anything that might grant me access. The night was cold and rain began to fall in sheets, and a gust of wind tugged at my clothes as if warning me away from the dark path I was determined to follow.

Focused on finding an entrance, I barely heard the rustle behind me until a firm hand clamped down on my shoulder. I spun around, my breath catching in my throat, to face the stern features of a security guard. The man's grip was iron, his expression unreadable beneath the brim of his cap.

"What do you think you're doing here, boy?" the guard demanded, his voice a low growl that matched his intimidating stance.

Caught off guard and fearing for my safety, I stammered an apology, trying to concoct a plausible reason for my presence. "I—I thought I heard someone in trouble," I managed, my voice shaking.

The guard's eyes narrowed, and he gave me a long, measuring look. "This is private property, and you're trespassing. Get out of here now, and don't let me catch you around again. Next time, you might find yourself locked inside. I know your parents, Steve and Margrett. I'll keep a room open just for them if I see your ass back here." With a forceful shove, he pushed me towards the gate.

The threat echoed ominously in my ears as I stumbled out onto the road, the gate clanging shut behind me. The promise of danger from the guard's words lingered with me as I made the quiet walk back home, the scenes I had witnessed burning bright and terrible in my mind.

Upon reaching my house, I found my parents in the living room, the TV casting flickering shadows across their concerned faces. "Ethan, where have you been?" my mother asked, noticing my disheveled appearance and the edge of urgency in my movements.

I took a deep breath, ready to unload everything I had seen—the chained man, the guard, the palpable sense of dread that hung over the asylum. But as I relayed my story, I could see the disbelief forming in my parents' eyes.

"Ethan, that place... you know it's troubled, but these stories... you must have been mistaken," my father interjected, a hint of warning in his tone. "It's dangerous, and poking around there isn't going to help anyone."

"But you didn't see what I saw," I insisted, frustration mounting. "There's something terrible happening there, and someone needs to do something about it."

My mother exchanged a worried glance with my father before responding, her voice firm yet fearful. "We know you want to help, but think about the consequences. If the Asylum closes down suddenly, where do you think all those patients will go? They'll be out here, in Talmage, with nowhere else to go."

The implication was clear: my parents feared the repercussions more than they were inclined to uncover any mistreatment. They wanted to maintain the status quo, to keep the unknown and the unwanted at a distance.

Deflated and frustrated, I excused myself and headed to my room. I had left for Chico State two years ago but always returned home during winter break. My room was kept just as it was when I finished my senior year at Ukiah High. My parents had told me that they would always keep my room empty just in case I needed to come home.

Growing up in Talmage, a town where everyone knew each other's business, I was always a bit of an outlier. In high school, my fascination with the morbid and the macabre marked me as different. I spent my weekends in the local library, pouring over books about alchemy, anatomy, and ancient burial rites, or roaming the edges of the nearby woods, imagining the land whispering its dark secrets.

Despite my unusual interests, I was never truly ostracized. This was largely thanks to my best friend, Mike, a star football player whose charisma and popularity shielded me from the brunt of teenage cruelty. Mike and I were an unlikely duo; his days were spent in rigorous practices and boisterous team meetings, while mine were lost in sketchbooks and horror novels. Yet, he respected my quirks, often standing firmly by my side if anyone dared to mock my gothic leanings. His unwavering loyalty was a rare comfort in the otherwise judgmental environment of high school.

After graduation, I took my passion for the chemical mysteries of the natural world to Chico State, where I decided to major in chemistry. It was 1969, and the cultural revolution was in full swing, with young people across the country pushing against the boundaries of the old world. Inspired by this spirit of rebellion and discovery, I dreamt of synthesizing LSD, not just for the hallucinogenic experience but also as an exploration into the profound and transformative properties of chemicals. I envisioned myself as a modern-day alchemist, turning mundane materials into substances that could expand the mind and alter perceptions.

My college days were a blur of experiments and theoretical studies, mixed with the colorful, psychedelic culture of the late '60s. I thrived in the academic environment, my earlier isolation transforming into an asset as my unique blend of interests and knowledge became valued among peers intrigued by the promise of psychedelics. My experiments in the lab were both a continuation of my childhood curiosity about the shadowy aspects of life and a concrete way to make my mark in a world that was rapidly changing.

Yet, despite my deep dive into the world of chemistry and my embrace of the counterculture swirling around me, the shadows of my youth in Talmage never fully receded. The old, eerie tales, the quiet murmurs of the unknown, and the dark corners of human experience continued to fascinate and haunt me. This enduring intrigue with the macabre would, unknowingly, prepare me for the twisted paths my life would take after my academic pursuits, drawing me inexorably back to the mysteries and shadows of Talmage, to the looming presence of River Road Asylum, and to the dark unraveling that awaited.

Lying in bed, I stared at the ceiling, my mind racing. The town's fear of the patients, my parents' unwillingness to intervene, the guard's ominous warning—all of it swirled in my head. But rather than deterring me, their disbelief and the threats only deepened my will to continue.

I couldn't let it go. I wouldn't. No matter what it took, I knew I had to return to the River Road Asylum. I had to find out the truth and expose whatever darkness lay within those walls.

Morning light filtered through the curtains of my room, casting long beams across my face. I had hardly slept, the images from last night haunting my restless dreams. With a heavy sigh, I rose from my bed, determined to find some answers. If my parents wouldn't believe me, maybe my friends would have some insights—or at least they wouldn't dismiss my concerns outright.

After a quick shower and grabbing my jacket, I headed to Fjord's, a local diner that had been a staple in Ukiah since before I could remember. The place smelled of strong coffee and fried bacon, a comforting scent that usually brought a sense of calm. Today, however, it did little to ease my tension.

I spotted some old friends, Mike and Sarah, sitting in their usual booth by the window. Mike had worked at the town's garage since graduating high school, a job that seemed to suit his mechanical genius. Sarah had gone off to college but ended up returning home after just one semester to help run her family's bookstore. Unlike me, they had no dreams of leaving the small town of Ukiah and were already woven into the fabric of the town.

"Hey," I greeted as I slid into the booth, my voice a mix of relief and urgency.

Mike looked up, his face etching with concern at my grave expression. "Ethan! I heard you were back in town. You look like you've seen a ghost, man. What's up?"

I glanced around before leaning in, lowering my voice. "It's about the asylum—River Road. I saw something last night... something bad. A man, chained up, bleeding... It's not right."

Sarah's eyes widened, a spark of fear flickering in them. "Ethan, you shouldn't mess with that place. It's... there's bad stuff happening there."

"Yeah," Mike chimed in, stirring his coffee absentmindedly. "It's not just rough stories; it's real. Some folks around town have been disappearing. Anyone who seems too curious or too vocal against the asylum... they just vanish."

My heart raced as their words confirmed my worst fears. "Do you think it's connected? The asylum, I mean?"

"I wouldn't doubt it," Sarah replied, her voice low. "Last month, Joan Turner—the journalist from the Talmage Times, remember her? She was working on an exposé about the asylum. The last anyone heard, she was digging up information on patient treatment and funding... Then, poof, gone. No one knows where she is now."

"And no one's really talking about it either," Mike added. "It's like they're scared. Scared of finding out the truth, scared of what happens when the truth comes out. And scared of what happens if the place shuts down. The patients, where do they go? What happens to them?"

I felt a fire building within me. "We can't just sit back and do nothing. We have to find out more, expose whatever is happening there."

Sarah bit her lip, thinking. "I know it's dangerous, Ethan, but you're right. We can't just ignore it. Maybe... maybe we can look into Joan's work, and see if she left anything behind at the paper. Anything that could tell us what she found."

"And I've got a buddy in the police department," Mike offered. "I can poke around, and see if there are any official reports or records about the disappearances."

Energized by their support, I nodded. "Let's do it. Let's find out what's really happening at the Asylum. We owe it to the town, to those patients, and ourselves."

We left Fjords with a plan forming, unaware of the eyes that watched us from across the street, the watcher's interest piqued by our not-so-quiet conversation. As we parted ways, each of us felt the weight of the task ahead, but also the strength of our decision to move forward. We were in this together, and we were determined to shine a light on the darkness at River Road Asylum.

As I delved deeper into the unsettling environment of the asylum, whispered rumors and vague warnings began to reach me, painting a picture filled with gaps I couldn't quite fill. Among the shadows of stories and frightened silences, one name emerged with an eerie frequency: Dr. Blackwell. The mention of him always seemed to draw dark clouds over any conversation, yet no one was willing to explain why.

The details were frustratingly sparse. Some of the townsfolk spoke of Dr. Blackwell in quiet murmurs, as if the very walls might be listening. Others simply changed the subject with an urgency that suggested fear more than disapproval. It was as if he had appeared out of thin air, with no past and a presence shrouded in ominous ambiguity. Curiosity pricked at me; why was his presence so disturbing to everyone here?

There were unsettling anecdotes, too—rumors of treatments that pushed far beyond the boundaries of modern medicine, described by those few willing to talk as if they were recounting horror stories beside a campfire. Stories abounded of patients who were never the same after entering his care, some supposedly disappearing without a trace. Was he a strict practitioner with unorthodox methods, or was there something more sinister at play?

The most unnerving aspect was not what was said, but what was left unsaid. The air of mystery that surrounded Dr. Blackwell suggested something deeper, darker—a malevolence that no one dared to confront directly. This ambiguity left a void filled with speculation: who was he really, and what was happening within the secluded wards of River Road?

Driven by these questions and the palpable fear that seemed to follow the mention of his name, I decided that I needed to learn more. Whether Dr. Blackwell was a misunderstood doctor or something far more troubling, it was clear that something unusual, perhaps dangerous, was happening. If there was a story here, it wasn't just about an asylum struggling under the weight of its legacy—it was about uncovering what Dr. Blackwell represented in this hidden world of whispers and shadows.

With Mike's insider access and Sarah's investigative prowess, we were poised to dig deeper into this mystery. Our next steps would have to be cautious. Whatever lay beneath the chilling tales of Dr. Blackwell, I was determined to uncover it, ready to shine a light on the darkness that lurked in the heart of River Road Asylum. The truth, however unsettling, needed to be revealed.

Dr. Blackwell

In a nondescript town in the northeastern United States, a series of disturbing events unfolded in the late 1950s that left the local community in a state of terror and confusion. Bodies were discovered in remote areas, each subjected to bizarre and precise surgical procedures that no known medical professional would dare claim as standard practice. The local newspapers dubbed the perpetrator "The Surgeon," due to the clinical precision of the incisions and the apparent knowledge of human anatomy demonstrated in the mutilations.

The Surgeon was, in reality, a young man by the name of Henry Blackwell, whose brilliance in medical school was matched only by his deepening fascination with the human body's limits and capabilities. Unbeknownst to his peers, Henry viewed the human body not as a temple but as a test subject for exploring pain thresholds and the impact of extreme surgical modifications on human physiology.

Dr. Henry Blackwell's experiments began in the shadows of his own home, where he lured the unsuspecting under the guise of free medical care. His methods grew increasingly radical and unsanctioned, driven by a belief that he was on the brink of a medical breakthrough that could redefine human understanding of pain and survival. However, as law enforcement began to connect the dots leading to his doorstep, Blackwell realized he needed a safer haven for his work—a place where his horrific experiments could continue under the protection of legitimacy.

In 1962, Dr. Blackwell stumbled upon an opening at River Road Asylum in California. It was a godsend for Blackwell—remote, isolated, and filled with society's forgotten souls. He assumed the identity of a compassionate psychiatrist dedicated to the treatment of the mentally ill, his impeccable credentials and charming demeanor quickly silencing any initial skepticism.

Once established at River Road Asylum, Dr. Blackwell took advantage of the asylum's autonomy and the lack of oversight that came with such institutions at the time. He portrayed himself as a pioneering doctor, introducing new "treatments" that were, in reality, continuations of his gruesome experiments. The patients, isolated from the world and stripped of their rights, became his unwilling subjects, trapped in a nightmare disguised as healthcare.

The asylum provided Dr. Blackwell with an endless supply of subjects and the perfect cover to carry out his dark ambitions. He established a special ward where his most secretive operations were conducted under the guise of cutting-edge therapeutic procedures. The screams that echoed through the halls were dismissed as the unfortunate but necessary sounds of healing by the disturbed.

As time passed, the body count and the whispers of misconduct grew, but Blackwell's manipulative charisma kept the horrors well hidden. Staff turnover was high, and those who suspected the truth were either too frightened to speak up or mysteriously disappeared before they could take their suspicions to the authorities.

Years wore on, and Dr. Blackwell's façade of the benevolent psychiatrist began to crack. Whispers turned into investigations, and the chilling reality began to surface. However, Blackwell was always one step ahead, his plans adapting and evolving to protect his life's work. When a young college student named Ethan, fascinated by the morbid and unknowingly connected to a deeper past of the town, took an interest in the asylum, Blackwell saw both a threat and an opportunity to pass on his legacy.

Unknown to Ethan and the rest of Talmage, they were living alongside a monster in plain sight, a predator masked as a healer, who had turned the River Road Asylum into a palace of pain and terror—a legacy that he was preparing to hand over to the next generation, willing or n ot.

As Dr. Henry Blackwell solidified his control over Talmage, the dark undercurrents of his past began to seep into the present. The chilling legacy he had left behind in the northeastern states started to manifest in the quiet, rolling landscapes surrounding Talmage. Hikers and hunters in the nearby mountains began stumbling upon gruesome scenes that seemed ripped from a nightmarish tale—bodies discovered in secluded areas, each marked by the surgical precision that had become the horrifying signature of Blackwell's earlier life as "The Surgeon."

These bodies were found partially buried under piles of leaves or hidden in shallow graves, their conditions speaking of a strange duality of care and carnage. The corpses exhibited meticulously executed incisions, organs either rearranged or missing entirely, with the thoracic cavities often left open, exposing rib cages that gleamed white against the decaying foliage. The local authorities, already under Blackwell's influence, were quick to cordon off the areas and dismiss the deaths as animal attacks or unfortunate accidents, despite the obvious signs of surgical intervention.

Whispers among the town's more skeptical residents speculated about the connection between these horrifying discoveries and the asylum's shadowy operations. Yet, these suspicions were spoken only in subdued conversations, for fear of retribution. The police, now ever more the enforcers of Blackwell's will, monitored conversations and movements with an intensity that stifled any serious investigations.

The fear induced by the mysterious deaths served Blackwell's purposes well. They reinforced his narrative about the dangers lurking outside the orderly society he promised to uphold. He utilized the town meetings to subtly remind the townsfolk of his indispensable role in maintaining their safety, often alluding to the unspoken threats that only he could mitigate. This tactic ensured that the community's dependence on him only deepened, binding Talmage to his sinister agenda even more tightly.

In private, Blackwell reveled in the terror that his hidden activities induced. It was not just about controlling the town or conducting his depraved experiments—it was also about the power to invoke fear. Each body found in the mountains was a message, a testament to his unchallenged dominion over life and death, a grim reminder of what could happen to those who dared to oppose him.

By late 1968, the number of mysterious deaths had subtly declined, but the fear they had engendered lingered, like a toxic mist that hung over the town. Blackwell, ever the opportunist, used this lull to introduce more extreme "therapeutic" techniques at the asylum, his public justifications couched in the language of necessity and protection. The town's leaders, their wills eroded by fear and manipulation, offered little resistance, their earlier doubts smothered under layers of coercion and resignation.

As Talmage approached the end of the decade, it stood as a town out of time, a community overshadowed by the looming asylum and haunted by the specter of a man who was both its savior and tormentor. The people of Talmage, caught in Blackwell's web, moved through their days with a wary resignation, their eyes avoiding the asylum's high walls and what they contained. Unbeknownst to them, they were not just residents of a small town but captives of a grand, dark experiment orchestrated by a mind twisted by visions of control and conquest. The stage was set, and Blackwell's rule was absolute, the town unwittingly complicit in the horrors hidden in plain sight.

The Plan

The chill of the evening air clung to me as I walked back to my house, the uneasy weight of the asylum's secrets heavy on my mind. I expected to return to the familiar warmth of home, to shake off the chill with a hot drink and discuss my next steps with my parents. Instead, I was met with a scene that dropped my heart into the pit of my stomach.

The front door was ajar, an unusual sight that instantly sent a wave of apprehension through me. Inside, the house was dimly lit, the usual hum of daily life eerily absent. My father was in the living room, his face etched with fury and despair, a combination I had never seen before.

"Where's Mom?" I asked, my voice barely above a whisper, fearing the answer.

He stopped pacing and turned to face me; his expression dark. "I told you something bad would happen if you went poking around that place. Now they've got your mother," he said, his voice thick with anger and fear.

"What? Who's got her? What happened?" My voice rose in panic as the implications of his words began to sink in.

"Someone took her, Ethan."

My father, a shadow of his usual self, passed me a crumpled piece of paper with his still shaking hand. He had found it pinned to the front door earlier that day, a harsh and terrifying confirmation that they had taken Mom. It was a direct message from Dr. Blackwell, no doubt—a chilling consequence of our whispered suspicions and growing questions about the asylum.

I unfolded the note, the paper feeling unnaturally cold in my hands. The message was clear, its menacing words written in a harsh, angular scrawl: "Stop looking or she's next." It was a direct threat, leveraging our worst fears against our desperate need to find my mom.

"This is my fault," I murmured, guilt washing over me like a tidal wave.

"No, it's not your fault," my father said, his voice softening as he saw my distress. "But we need to be smart now. We need to do as he said or we'll never see her again."

I nodded, my anger beginning to boil over. The fear for my mother's safety propelled me into action. "I'm going back there. I'm going to bring down the son of a bitch who's behind this and bring Mom home."

"Ethan, it's too dangerous," my father protested, but I could see in his eyes that he knew as well as I did that it was the only way.

"I need to do this, Dad. For Mom. I have Mike and Sarah—they'll help. We're not going in unprepared," I assured him, trying to inject confidence I only half-felt. "I'm calling them right now."

The cold, sterile click of the rotary dial echoed through the quiet house as I reached for our brand-new, canary-yellow Western Electric phone. The deliberate motion of spinning the dial, the mechanical whirl and slow, dragging return of each number felt agonizingly slow, each rotation amplifying my anxiety. My fingers trembled slightly as I entered Mike's number, the familiar sequence now a lifeline in the growing storm of my fears.

"Mike!" I blurted out the moment I heard the line pick up, my voice tight with urgency. "You need to get over here right now." The words tumbled out, a rush of desperate energy.

"What's up, man? Slow down. Are you okay?" Mike's voice came through, tinged with concern but still too calm, too removed from the immediacy of my panic.

"No, I—I'm not okay," I admitted, my voice cracking slightly under the strain. "Can you call Sarah and have her come over too? It's bad, man. Just get over here," I insisted, the gravity of the situation compressing the air around me, making it thick and hard to breathe.

The receiver clacked heavily back into its cradle, the impact sending a sharp ring echoing back through the handset, a somber bell tolling for the urgency of the moment. I cast a lingering, worried glance at my dad, his form slouched in his usual chair, oblivious to the turmoil swirling around him. With heavy steps, I retreated to my room to await my friends' arrival, each step seeming to echo my racing heart.

The dim glow of the lamp in the living room cast long shadows against the walls, the room draped in a gloomy, uneasy light. Outside, the fog pressed against the windows like a smothering blanket, the world beyond a blur of obscured shapes and muffled sounds.

When Mike and Sarah finally arrived, they burst through the door with a gust of damp, chilled air, their faces etched with lines of concern. They paused just inside the threshold, their eyes darting back to the fog-shrouded night as if expecting some form of the dread I'd hinted at to materialize from the mist.

"Tell us everything," Mike said, closing the door behind him, the sound sealing us off from the oppressive atmosphere outside. Sarah nodded her expression grave, both of them bracing themselves against the weight of the unknown crisis they had stepped into. The room, with its lingering echoes of normalcy, now felt like the fragile calm at the eye of an impending storm.

Mike leaned over to read the note as I held it out. "He knows we've been talking, Ethan," he said, his voice grim. "This isn't just a warning; it's a move to silence us."

Sarah nodded, her eyes wide with fear. "They left this when they took your mom. Blackwell is playing a dangerous game. He's watching us, maybe even listening."

The reality that our casual observations and discussions might have put my mother directly in harm's way was suffocating. My mind raced as I tried to piece together our previous conversations, the casual mentions of odd happenings at the asylum spoken too loudly in public spaces, or phone calls perhaps intercepted. It was a network of paranoia, but now it felt justified.

"What do we do now?" I asked, my voice barely above a whisper as if the walls of my own home might betray us. "We can't just do nothing. My mom—she could be..."

"We need to act, but carefully," Mike interjected, his strategic mind mapping out our precarious path forward. "Going against Blackwell directly is too risky, especially now. He's made it clear he won't hesitate to escalate things."

Sarah paced the room, then stopped, turning to face us. "We should get help, but from outside Talmage. Someone Blackwell can't touch. Maybe a private investigator or even the FBI, if it comes to that. Someone who can start looking into this without the same risks we face."

The idea of bringing in outside help felt like a lifeline in the darkness that had descended upon us. We agreed to keep our actions and discussions even more guarded, using code words in our communications and meeting only in person, away from possible electronic surveillance.

As Mike and Sarah prepared to leave, we huddled together for a moment, the weight of our shared secret binding us more tightly than ever. "Be careful," I murmured as they stepped back out into the fog, which seemed to swallow them whole, leaving only the echo of their footsteps behind.

Just as they were about to head out, a horrifying sound shattered the night—tires squealing aggressively outside. We rushed to the front door just in time to see a car speeding away into the darkness. There, in the glow of the streetlights, lay a figure bound and motionless.

It was my mother.

We ran to her, my father and I, our hearts pounding in terror. As we reached her, the sight that met us was freakish and unbearable—her lips were missing, her tongue removed, her mouth a gaping, bloodied horror. Nailed to her forehead was a note, the words scrawled in a taunting crawl: "Go ahead, Ethan, keep digging."

The world spun around me as I cradled her head in my hands, the note's message burning into my mind. It had to be Dr. Blackwell who did this, and he wasn't just warning us; he was challenging us, daring us to uncover the truth, no matter the cost. As I looked into my father's eyes, we shared a silent vow. This was far from over. The horrors of River Road Asylum had come to our doorstep, and now, more than ever, we needed to bring them to light. We needed justice, not just for my mother, but for all the silent voices echoing through the halls of that forsaken place.

Mothers Revenge

As my father rushed inside to call 911, the sound of his frantic voice echoed sharply against the walls of our home. The night air felt thick with dread as we waited, my mother's body lying still on the cold pavement, a brutal reminder of the dangers we were meddling with. The minutes dragged, each second heavier than the last until finally, the wail of sirens cut through the stillness of the night, and the flashing lights of the police cars bathed the street in red and blue.

Officers and paramedics descended upon our home with urgency, yet their eyes avoided meeting mine, as if my family's misfortune was a contagion they feared catching. They worked quickly to secure the area, their professionalism a thin veil over the underlying tension. As they prepared to haul my mother's body away, the gravity of the situation sank in, her absence a hollow space beside me that echoed with every heartbeat.

One of the officers, a stocky man with a stern face, pulled me aside as his colleagues continued their grim duties. His grip on my arm was tight, his voice low and menacing. "See what fucking happens when you stir shit up. Go back to Chico where you belong," he hissed, his breath reeking of disdain.

I stared at him; my grief momentarily replaced by a surge of anger. How could he blame me for the cruelty and madness inflicted by others? But as his cold eyes bore into mine, I realized that this was more than just a warning. It was a message, perhaps from the very heart of the darkness I was trying to expose.

"I'm not going anywhere," I replied firmly, my voice steadier than I felt. "This is my home, and I will take down the asshole who did this to my mother."

The officer scoffed, a sound muffled by the commotion around us, and released my arm. He turned away without another word, but his message was clear: my pursuit of the truth was not welcome here, and my family had paid a horrifying price for my tenacity.

As the ambulance drove away with my mother, the reality of our situation settled in like a weight in my chest. I could feel the eyes of the community on me—some pitying, some accusatory. It was clear that my investigation had provoked forces more dangerous and far-reaching than I had anticipated.

Determined more than ever, I turned to Mike and Sarah, their faces etched with concern. "We can't let this stop us," I told them, my voice fueled by a mix of fear and defiance. "Whatever is happening at the River Road

Asylum, it's bigger than we thought. They wouldn't go this far if there wasn't something major to hide."

Mike nodded, clenching his fists. "We're with you, Ethan. All the way," he said, his determination matching my own.

Sarah placed a hand on my shoulder, her touch gentle yet firm. "Let's do this right. For your mom, for all the victims. We need to be smart, and thorough. Let's gather more evidence and expose these bastards."

As the shadows lengthened into the late afternoon, we found ourselves immersed in a grim discourse. There we were, plotting the downfall of the institution that had woven such a tapestry of suffering and terror. Despite the leaps of modern medicine, it baffled me why such a nefarious place was permitted to exist. My thoughts were a silent storm as Sarah rose from the faded grass of the front lawn, brushing off her jeans in a futile attempt to shed the clinging blades.

"Mike, could you drive me home?" she asked, her voice weary, tinged with the weight of our purpose. She shook her head slowly, a gesture of resignation mixed with purpose. "Ethan, I'm so sorry about your mom. We're going to get these bastards."

Mike heaved himself to his feet, stretching until his back cracked—a reminder of his glory days as Ukiah High's football star, now just echoes in his strained sinews. "All right, Sarah, let's hit the road. Ethan, she's right. We're going to take these damned bastards down."

"Thanks, you guys. I appreciate all the help," I managed, though inside, fear gnawed at me like a ravenous beast. The notion haunted me that one of us might be next. It felt as if the entire town's eyes were upon us, their ears catching every whisper. A collective breath held, as if they all wished to silence our cries into the encroaching dusk.

As Mike and Sarah climbed into Mike's gleaming new 1969 Chevy C-10, I stepped up onto the porch, feeling the weight of the evening's uncertainties. I lingered there, watching as the truck's headlights cut through the thickening dusk, the rumble of the engine briefly disrupting the evening's silence. With a last sweep of gravel under tires, they backed out of the driveway, and the red taillights blinked momentarily before disappearing into the night.

Turning, I crossed the threshold back into the house. The door shut behind me with a definitive click, and the sudden silence enveloped me. It was a lonely, heavy quiet that seemed almost tangible, pressing in around me like a dense, suffocating blanket. The familiar spaces of the home felt strangely alien, charged with a stillness that was both calming and unnervingly oppressive. The dim light from the hallway added a ghostly quality to the room as the echo of my friends' departure faded into the encroaching night.

My father was ensconced in his threadbare easy chair, the one that had molded to his weary frame over the years, eyes fixed on an episode of "Gunsmoke" yet distant, lost in a deeper, darker reverie.

"Pops, I'm so sorry about mom. I can't believe they would do something like that." The words felt heavy in the muted glow of the television.

He turned slowly, his gaze meeting mine, wrestling with the tumult of his thoughts. I could see the storm of sorrow behind his stern façade, the urge to surrender to tears, but his rugged exterior held firm, a dam against the grief. With a slight nod, he looked away, his gaze returning to the flickering images on the screen, his silence a palpable presence in the room.

"I'll talk to you in the morning, Dad. You should try to get some rest. If you need anything, I'll be in my room," I said, retreating into the quietude of the house, leaving him to his solemn vigil with the ghosts that danced in the blue television light.

I tried to find comfort in the familiar surroundings of my room, but every shadow seemed to whisper secrets, and every creak of the old wooden frame echoed like a scream in the darkness. Lying in bed, the image of my mother's mutilated body invaded my thoughts relentlessly. I imagined the terror she must have felt, the agony of her final moments. It was a mental torture chamber from which I could find no escape.

Exhaustion finally overcame me, and I drifted into a troubled sleep. The dreams that visited me were vivid and disturbing—echoes of my mother's pain mingled with faceless threats lurking in every shadow. I awoke with a start to the shrill ring of the telephone, cutting through the silence like a warning siren.

Heart pounding, I rushed to the kitchen, the phone's cord trailing behind me as I dragged it back to my room. "Hello. Who is this?" I asked, my voice shaky.

"It's me, Ethan, it's Mike. They got Sarah. This morning, I found a note on my door that said, 'Come to the Asylum if you want your friend back.' I gotta go to work, but I'm coming over to your place tonight. I'll be there at seven o'clock." The line went dead before I could respond.

At exactly seven o'clock, Mike appeared at my doorstep, his complexion ghostly, his hands trembling slightly as he held the note. His eyes flickered nervously, scanning the dimming corners of the porch as though he feared the gathering shadows might animate and attack. "I got a weird phone call too," he whispered, his voice dropping to a near whisper, laden with urgency. He leaned closer, instinctively lowering his voice further, as if afraid that the very air around us might betray his words. "They warned me—if we talk to anyone about going to the asylum, others will end up hurt... or worse."

The weight of his words hung between us, a tangible presence that seemed to darken the room. We sat in silence, the gravity of the situation pressing down upon us. It was clear now that what we faced was no mere scandal to be uncovered; it was a malevolent force, willing to maim, kill, and terrorize to keep its secrets buried.

Determination hardened in my voice as I faced Mike. "We have to go," I declared, the firmness in my tone belying the chaos churning inside me. "We can't let them do to Sarah what they did to my mom."

Mike nodded, his expression grim yet resolute. "I agree, but let's try calling the FBI before we head out. That way, at least they'll know where to look if we go missing," he suggested. His leadership qualities, evident since the day we met, had always instilled a sense of confidence and direction in our group. If anyone could steer us through this nightmare, it was Mike.

"Let's use the payphone down the road, just in case the asylum has our phones tapped," I added, the edges of my voice tinged with paranoia. "We don't need them targeting my dad too." He was all I had left, and the thought of drawing any danger his way was unbearable.

Without informing my dad of our plans—a decision made easier by his distant, preoccupied demeanor—we quietly slipped out the front door. The night air was cool and carried a mist that clung to our clothes as we walked. Talmage Road was quiet, the silence punctuated only by our hurried footsteps as we made our way to the local convenience store where the old, weather-beaten payphone stood like a sentinel at the edge of reality and fear.

The bitter cold clung to us like a shroud as we huddled in the dim light of the neglected payphone booth. Mike's fingers trembled as he flipped through the worn pages of the phonebook, the brittle paper rasping under his touch. He located the number for the FBI, his movements quick and desperate. As he lifted the receiver, his breath visible in the chilly air, a tense silence enveloped us, broken only by the distant howl of the wind.

Mike dialed the number, each beep echoing ominously in the small booth. His face, illuminated by the faint glow of the streetlamp, was a mask of concentration and fear. After a moment that felt like an eternity, the line clicked, and the sound that came through was not the professional greeting we had anticipated but a voice chillingly familiar.

"Good evening, gentlemen," Dr. Blackwell's voice oozed through the receiver, smooth and menacing. "How can I assist you this fine night?"

The blood drained from Mike's face as he listened, his eyes widening in horror. I watched him, feeling a knot of dread tightening in my stomach. When Mike spoke, his voice was barely a whisper, "Blackwell, you monster, what have you done with Sarah?"

Dr. Blackwell chuckled, a sound that seemed to crawl deep under my skin. "Ah, Sarah, such a curious subject. She's currently assisting me in some very... advanced research. You see, her anatomy is proving quite enlightening. We're exploring pain thresholds tonight. Did you know the human body can survive far beyond the usual limits when properly motivated?"

Mike's hand clenched around the receiver, knuckles white. "What are you doing to her, you sick bastard?"

"Oh, just a few modifications," Blackwell's voice continued, dripping with mock concern. "A little alteration to her sad face, perhaps some enhancements to the nervous system. I find the screams quite educational."

I grabbed the receiver from Mike, my voice thick with rage and despair. "We're coming for her, Blackwell. This ends tonight!"

"By all means, come over," Blackwell replied, his tone taunting. "I always appreciate more volunteers. And should you choose to delay, remember, each moment you waste... Sarah gets to enjoy more of my life-altering treatments."

The line went dead, leaving us in a stunned silence. Mike looked at me, his face a ghastly pale in the moonlight, marked by a tenacity born of desperation. "We have to go, Ethan. Now. We can't let him continue... whatever hell he's putting her through."

Nodding, I felt a surge of adrenaline cut through the shock. Our plan to reach out for help had backfired disastrously, leaving us with no choice but to confront Blackwell directly at the asylum. The weight of his words, the graphic horror of his threats against Sarah, galvanized us into action.

With unwavering commitment, we set off toward the asylum, now envisioned in our minds as a bastion of untold horrors. The night seemed to tighten around us with each forward step, pulling us deeper into what we anticipated would be a harrowing ordeal. There was no option to turn back. Driven by a potent mix of fear, anger, and a desperate hope to rescue Sarah, we ventured through the enveloping darkness, the daunting reality of what awaited us at the asylum gnawing at our spirits.

The night had a sinister quality as Mike and I left the relative safety of the payphone booth, stepping onto the long, straight road that led to River Road Asylum. The road stretched out before us like a dark ribbon, the building's imposing silhouette growing larger with each step we took. The air was chillingly still, punctuated only by the occasional rustle of dry leaves skittering across the asphalt, their scraping a ghostly whisper in the eerie silence.

As we walked, every gust of wind felt like a cold breath on the back of our necks, a ghostly reminder of the danger we were walking into. Our footsteps were a steady crunch on the gravel, the rhythmic sound a small comfort in the oppressive quiet of the night.

"This road feels like it's leading straight to hell," Mike muttered, his voice low and tense.

I glanced at him, feeling the weight of our decision. "Maybe it is. But if it's the only way to save Sarah and get justice for my mom, then it's a road we have to walk."

We trudged on, each step seeming to draw the asylum nearer, its dark windows and towering spires silhouetted against the night sky like some ancient, malevolent entity. The structure loomed ever larger, its oppressive presence a physical weight that seemed to squeeze the very air around us.

"Do you think we'll even make it out of there?" Mike asked his voice a mix of fear and defiance.

I kept my eyes on the looming facade. "I don't know. But if things go south, I... I just want you to know, I couldn't have done this without you, man."

Mike nodded, a bleak smile flickering across his face. "Right back at you. And hey, if we go down, we go down fighting, right?"

"Right," I agreed, though the thought did little to ease the knot of apprehension in my stomach.

As we neared the gates of the asylum, the night seemed to close in tighter around us. The sounds of the countryside had fallen away, leaving only the echo of our footsteps and the pounding of our hearts in our ears.

"We might not both make it out of this," I said quietly, stopping for a moment to look at Mike. "If anything happens to me, try to keep going. Make sure people find out what's been happening here."

Mike clapped a hand on my shoulder, his grip firm. "Only if you promise to do the same. But let's not write the end of our story just yet, huh? We've still got a chance to rewrite this fucked up night.."

Nodding, we faced the gates of the asylum together. The air was colder here, the darkness deeper. It felt as though we were standing on the threshold of another world, a realm ruled by madness and shadow.

Taking a deep breath, we pushed the gates open. They creaked ominously, a sound that seemed to echo into the depths of the night, announcing our arrival. With a shared glance, we stepped forward, crossing into the grounds of the asylum, our determination fortified by the knowledge of what was at stake.

A guard met us, his presence chilling in the dim light. He gave us a shit-eating grin that didn't quite reach his eyes and said, "Welcome to the party. I think this is one you'll never want to leave from." His eerie laugh echoed behind us as we walked inside, making the hairs on my neck stand up.

Inside, the atmosphere was suffocating, the shadows seeming to pulsate with a life of their own. The corridors stretched endlessly; their corners shrouded in darkness that even flashlights would be reluctant to penetrate. It was as if the building itself was alive, watching us, breathing along with a slow, deliberate malice.

As we cautiously moved forward, a voice suddenly crackled over the PA system, cold and omnipresent, "Follow the trail of blood and bile. If you don't look hard, you may be here a while." The voice was followed by a low, mocking laughter that faded into a static hiss.

Swallowing hard, I looked over at Mike. "What the fuck did we get ourselves into?"

Mike looked back my way with a half-cocked smile and shook his head. "I don't know man, but we're in it now."

The command was horrifying, but it gave us a direction. With a deep, steadying breath, we began our search, following the chilling instruction. The floors were marred with dried streaks of dark blood that led deeper into the heart of the asylum. Each step felt heavy, each breath labored, as we traced the chilling path laid out before us.

As we advanced, the asylum began to unveil its chilling secrets through hushed whispers and lurking shadows. The walls bore scars—some scratches were new, glistening faintly in the dim light, while others were old, their edges worn by time, each one a silent testament to long-suffered despair and madness. Eerie sounds floated to our ears as we moved deeper—occasionally a muffled thud, sometimes a faint whimper—evidence of tormented souls that still dwelled within these confines. Some were trapped forever within the cold, unyielding walls, others still haunted by their nightmares, hidden just beyond each closed door we passed.

As we delved deeper, the atmosphere grew increasingly oppressive. It felt as though the air itself was laden with the accumulated echoes of pain and fear that had permeated the very stones of the building. Shadows around us appeared to twitch with potential movement, each sound suggesting the presence of unseen watchers or lingering spirits. The sense of dread was almost tangible, a heavy, suffocating force that seemed intent on crushing our willpower from every side.

Yet, the thought of Sarah, somewhere ahead, possibly enduring horrors we could barely imagine, spurred us onward. We were deep within the belly of the beast now, and there was no choice but to press forward, to confront whatever lay at the end of this gruesome trail. The terror was almost overwhelming, but our mission was clear. We had to find Sarah, uncover the truth of this dreadful place, and somehow, find a way out again.

Sarah's Happy Place

As Mike and I delved deeper into the chilling corridors of River Road Asylum, each echoing scream that filled the air was a bleak reminder that even though it was 1969, places like this still operated on the fringes of medical ethics. The cries of the inmates were real and immediate, a horrifying soundtrack, where the line between treatment and torment was dangerously blurred.

The air inside was thick with the antiseptic sting typical of such facilities, undercut by a more sinister undercurrent of decay and despair. These were the halls of a fully functional asylum, a relic from the late 1800s when psychiatric care was often primitive and brutal, and the cries of the suffering were all too common.

We approached the main dining hall, a cavernous room designed to hold the many souls unlucky enough to find themselves confined there. It was here that we saw Sarah. Positioned deliberately at the head of the table to face us as we entered, her appearance was gut-wrenching. Her eyes, hollow and devoid of the spark they once held, stared back at us emptily. A trickle of blood from one eye stained her cheek, while her mouth had been shockingly carved into a permanent, jagged smile, exposing all her teeth in a grimace that spoke of unimaginable pain.

An elderly-looking man in a white doctor's coat, wearing a black smiley face mask, stood by her side, embodying the twisted spirit of the era's less scrutinized psychiatric practices. "Welcome to the party," he announced through the mask, his voice chillingly calm and merry. "I think this is one you'll never want to leave."

His casual touch on Sarah's shoulder as he greeted us was a grotesque parody of reassurance. The guards stationed by the door watched impassively, their expressions unreadable behind their masks of duty.

This horrifying scene underscored the dark reality of our mission. River Road Asylum was not a relic of horrors past but a living, breathing entity where atrocities against the human psyche were committed daily. The cries echoing through the walls and screams seeming to crawl under the door were a testament to just how cruel and unusual this place was.

As the eerie, welcoming words of the masked doctor echoed through the dining hall, Mike's face contorted with a mixture of rage and desperation. He made a sudden move toward Sarah, his instinct to protect her overwhelming his caution. "Sarah!" he shouted, his voice breaking with emotion.

But before he could reach her, the man in the white coat, swift and chillingly precise, stepped forward and jammed a needle into Mike's neck. Mike's legs buckled beneath him, and he collapsed to the floor, his body going limp almost instantly. The room spun into a horrifying silence for a moment, the only sound, was Mike's shallow, labored breathing.

The doctor turned his masked face towards me, his bloodshot eyes cold and calculating behind the black smiley. "Sit down," he commanded, gesturing to the chair opposite Sarah with an unsettling calmness. His voice was smooth, betraying none of the violence of his actions.

"I hope you like the work I've done with your friend. I took some artistic liberties, she's so happy now."

"Why are you doing all this?"

"I just want everyone to understand how important our work here is. Soon everyone will be just as happy as Sarah. Guards, go ahead and take Mike here and get him prepped for surgery."

"No," I screamed as I began stepping forward to stop the men from taking another one of my friends away. I hesitated, my heart pounding in my chest, but the sharp click of a gun being cocked from one of the guards reminded me of the precariousness of our situation.

"Now, sit the Fuck down! Sorry excuse my tone. Can we sit down and have a nice meal, please? You're our special guest tonight. Sarah got all dressed up, just look how happy she is to see you."

With a heavy heart and a mind racing for any solution, I complied, moving slowly to the designated chair and sitting down. The coldness of the metal felt like ice against my skin, a harsh contrast to the heat of my fear and anger.

Across from me, Sarah's eyes met mine. Though her face was crudely frozen into that hacked smile, a single tear managed to escape, rolling down her blood-stained cheek. It was a silent testament to her agony and a poignant reminder of the brutal reality she endured. Despite the gruesome disfigurement, her eyes still communicated a depth of fear and sorrow that words could never capture.

The masked doctor watched our exchange with a perverse kind of glee. "Now, isn't this better?" he taunted. "We're all together now, just like a family." His laugh was hollow, resonating off the walls of the dining hall.

"What do you want from us?" I managed to choke out, my voice steady despite the tumult of emotions inside me.

"Oh, it's not what I want from you," the doctor replied, his tone mockingly contemplative. "It's about what you want from me. You came here looking for answers, didn't you? Well, you're about to get more than you bargained f or."

He paced slowly in front of us, hands clasped behind his back, the needle still in one hand. "You see, this institution isn't just about containment or even treatment. It's about control, about breaking down the human spirit until there's nothing left but obedience. And you, my dear intruders, have disrupted our harmony."

The threat in his voice was palpable, and it was clear that escaping from this twisted scenario was not going to be straightforward. The asylum was his domain, and we were caught in his web now, far deeper and more dangerous than I had ever anticipated. Every scream that echoed through those halls, every cry of torment, was a piece of this horrifying puzzle we had stumbled into. Now, it was up to me to find a way out, not just for my own sake, but for Sarah, Mike, and every soul trapped within these walls.

The room filled with a palpable tension as the doctor, with a grandiose flourish of his hand, called out, "Bring forth the feast." The sound of the double doors swinging open reverberated through the dining hall, and in walked a team of chefs, each dressed in immaculate white uniforms, pushing carts topped with gleaming silver platters. The surreal normalcy of their appearance clashed violently with the grisly setting of the asylum.

They positioned the carts around the stainless-steel table where I sat frozen, the atmosphere thick with an unspeakable dread. With mechanical precision, each chef lifted an ornate lid from their platter, revealing the contents underneath. My stomach churned violently as my eyes took in the horrific sight—Human lips. Which I quickly pieced together, must be Sarah, displayed as if they were a delicacy, accompanied by what appeared to be a human hand, artfully drizzled with Bolognese sauce. The addition of a garnish of lettuce and a slice of orange did nothing to diminish the ghastliness of the meal; it only served to deepen the depravity of the scene before me.

The doctor, his presence looming ever larger as he presided over the table, lifted his mask just enough to expose his mouth. He smacked his lips with an eagerness that was chilling, his voice unnervingly cheerful as he urged, "What are you waiting for, eat up! It's not that bad. Might be a little chewy but if you squeeze a little orange, it slides right down the throat."

His words echoed harshly in the hollow dining hall, a hair-raising invitation that was impossible to accept. I felt a surge of nausea and horror, coupled with an overwhelming impulse to flee, to reject this nightmare unfolding around me. Yet, the armed guards by the doors and the doctor's watchful eyes reminded me of the forbidding reality—that escape was not an option, at least not yet.

"Please," I found myself saying again, my voice barely a whisper, "why are you doing this? Can't you just let me and my friends go?"

The doctor replaced his mask fully, concealing any hint of human expression as he responded with a tone that suggested he was explaining a simple, mundane fact. "It's all part of the therapy, my dear guest. Here, we believe in total immersion, in confronting the darkest appetites of the human psyche to cleanse it. You sought horror, you sought truth—what better way to understand than to partake in the deepest fears that one can imagine?"

I looked at the space where Mike, once lay unconscious on the floor, and then to Sarah, her eyes hollow yet filled with silent tears, and I knew that this man was beyond reasoning, beyond any semblance of humanity. The asylum, this cursed feast, was his playground, a realm where he reigned with cruelty masked as treatment.

Gathering every ounce of my strength, I realized that playing into his hands further would do us no good. I needed a plan, a way to turn this horrific situation to my advantage, to escape and bring down this madness. The solution would not come easily or without cost, but the alternative—participation in this bizzare charade—was unthinkable. As the doctor awaited my compliance, I nodded slowly, feigning a calm I did not feel, buying time as my mind raced for any viable escape route.

The dining hall, already suffused with a demented atmosphere, seemed to tighten around us as the doctor's command reverberated through the chilling space. "I said eat!" His voice was no longer cloaked in mock civility but had taken on a sharp, commanding edge that cut through the tense air.

"I'm not eating this shit! Sarah, I'm going to get us out of here. I promise," I declared, my voice steady despite the pounding fear in my chest. The words felt hollow, unsure, yet it was all I could offer in the face of such barbarity.

In response, the doctor's patience snapped visibly. He slammed his wrinkly white fists onto the table, the force of the impact causing the silver plates to jump and clatter. The sound echoed like crashing cymbals, rattling through my head, each clang a jarring reminder of our dire situation. His eyes, visible only through the slits of his mask, burned with a frenzied intensity.

The Game of Life

"You're not going anywhere. If we can't sit down and have a nice meal as a family, then we'll just move on to the entertainment portion of the evening," he growled menacingly. Turning his head slightly, he barked an order to the guards stationed ominously by the door, "Guards, go ahead and prep our guest who decided to sleep during our introductions."

At his words, a cold shiver of dread ran through my body. Two of the guards nodded grimly and exited the room, their steps heavy and foreboding. The remaining guard's grip on his baton tightened his stance alert, watching us with hawk-like scrutiny.

The doctor's twisted game was unfolding with morbid clarity. This was no mere dinner; it was a spectacle, a display of his complete control and derangement, staged for his perverse amusement. Around us, the shadows of the dining hall seemed to creep closer, as if drawn by the dark spectacle, the walls themselves bearing witness to yet another chapter of horror within the asylum's history.

With a chilling calmness, the doctor pulled a chair from under the table and sat down directly opposite me, his gaze never leaving my face. "Now, let's not be rude to our host," he said, his voice dripping with false courtesy that belied the malice underneath. "We have quite a show planned for tonight, and you, my dear guest, will play a pivotal role."

His words hung heavy in the air, a sinister promise of the horror yet to come. I glanced at Sarah, whose expression remained unnaturally fixed due to the cruel alterations to her face, yet her eyes—a clear window to her terror—communicated everything. Another tear managed to escape, trailing down her distorted cheek, a silent plea for an end to this nightmare.

As the moments ticked by, the heavy thud of returning footsteps signaled the guards' return. The door swung open, and they re-entered, dragging between them a new, struggling figure—a fellow patient, perhaps, or another unfortunate soul caught in the doctor's deadly web. The sight reignited the fury within me, a burning eagerness to end this madness.

I knew that whatever lay ahead, our only chance of survival lay in defiance and possibly turning the doctor's game against him. As the new victim was forcefully positioned at the center of the room, the doctor clapped his hands with glee, oblivious to the mounting tension. "Let the games begin," he announced, and the room plunged into a deeper silence, the kind that precedes a storm.

Dr. Blackwell paced leisurely before me, his expression one of contemplative malice. The glaring light of the dining hall threw his elongated shadow across the cold, tiled floor, making him appear more monstrous than man.

"Ethan," he began, his voice unnervingly calm as he stopped and faced me squarely, "your father has been quite the curious man tonight. Unfortunately for him, curiosity can sometimes lead to... undesirable outcomes." He gestured casually towards where my father was bound, his tone dripping with faux regret.

"See, he was found prowling around the grounds," Blackwell continued, his eyes narrowing slightly as he relished recounting the tale. "Asking questions of your whereabouts, looking in places he shouldn't have. Normally, I'd admire such tenacity, but in Talmage, it can be quite hazardous."

He paused, circling closer, his gaze fixed intently on me. "I respected your father, Ethan. Truly, I did. That's why your family has remained untouched all these years. Out of respect, nothing more." The sinister smile that crept across his face belied the coldness in his eyes. "But then you began to get a little too curious, didn't you? Stirring the pot, digging into matters that you know nothing about."

Dr. Blackwell leaned in, his face uncomfortably close to mine, the smell of Old Spice mingling with the faint odor of something rotten that seemed to emanate from his being. "I find it a rather tragic twist of fate. You, poking around, and now your father, poking into the darkest corners of my work. It seems only fitting that you both share in the consequences of such reckless curiosity."

Straightening up, he stepped back and gestured grandly to the dimly lit expanse of the hall. "So here we are, in the heart of my domain, where I reshape the fabric of human frailty into something... educative. You've forced my hand, Ethan. Now, I must show you exactly what happens to those who pry into realms they should avoid."

His voice took on a darker edge, a sharp contrast to the clinical detachment he had displayed earlier. "Tonight, you'll both participate in a demonstration of what I've been perfecting here. Consider it a crash course in the limits of human endurance and the enlightening power of pain."

The cold, clinical way Dr. Blackwell spoke about such horrors, as if discussing a mundane scientific experiment, sent a wave of dread crashing through me. It was clear that his respect for my father had boundaries, and those had been irrevocably crossed the moment our family's curiosity intersected with his dark ambitions. Now, trapped within the walls of his ghastly theater, the price of our inquisitiveness was about to be exacted in the most gruesome of lessons.

The air was thick with a palpable dread that seemed to cling to my skin as I frantically called out, "Dad! NO! You son of a bitch. Let my dad go. You can keep me here, just let him go." The words barely left my lips before a sharp pain exploded at the back of my head, sending me spiraling into darkness. The world vanished, swallowed by an abrupt and suffocating black.

I was jolted awake by the harsh, grating squeal of the PA system, its loud echo bouncing off the cold, unyielding walls of the asylum. A twisted voice crackled through, its tone mockingly cheerful, "I know most families like a board game, but our family is a little different if you couldn't tell. What I have for tonight is a spin on the old classic, which I call, "The Endgame of Life."

Groaning, I forced myself up to my knees, my head throbbing with each pulse of my frantic heartbeat. The scene that unfolded before my eyes froze the blood in my veins. There, directly in front of me, lay my father, his wrists and ankles cruelly held down to the cold stainless-steel table with dark brown leather straps. His chest heaved with shallow, labored breaths; a piece of paper ominously titled "The Endgame of Life" placed on his chest beneath the haunting words "Game Rules."

As I reached out a trembling hand to grasp the paper, a low moan escaped from my father. "Dad! Are you okay? I'm going to get us out of here, I promise." His eyes, sutured shut, knowingly filled with a mix of pain and desperation, met mine. He strained to lift his head, his movements weak and futile. He tried to gesture towards his mouth, but his arms were cruelly stretched out, shackled tight by the unforgiving leather.

Opening his mouth in an attempt to speak, the horrific reality of his condition became sickeningly clear. His teeth had been savagely pulled out, his mouth filling with blood that dribbled and spilled over his lips with each attempt to cough. The blood sprayed into the air in a fine mist, settling in small, droplets against the sterile shine of the table.

The sickening mutilation, the cold steel of the table, the harsh, clinical light casting deep shadows—all of it conspired to create a scene from the darkest corner of a nightmare. Here, in this twisted version of familial bonds, the game the doctor proposed was one of survival, twisted choices, and horrific sacrifices.

The voice over the PA system crackled again, pulling me back from the edge of despair with its sinister cheer. "Let's begin, shall we? Please, read the rules carefully. We wouldn't want to play the game wrong, after all."

Terror, raw and consuming, coursed through me as I clutched the rules, my hands shaking. Each word I read sank like a stone into the pit of my stomach, outlining this evil game where the stakes were painfully real, and the consequences of each move were potentially lethal. I had to think, to use whatever wits I had left to navigate this morbid game and save my father. The nightmare had only just begun, and every second counted in this perverse twist on family game night.

As I stared down at the chilling gameplay instructions, my heart hammered against my chest. The rules were clear yet horrifyingly vague, a twisted manipulation of choice and consequence. The words on the paper seemed to taunt me, each letter a sinister whisper in the cold, echoing room. "Okay, first; you must decide in this life if you would like to have friends or family. Choose wisely because just like in life the decisions you make may come back to haunt you."

"Shit. What does that mean? What does that mean?" I muttered under my breath, panic setting in. The choices presented were impossible, a cruel game designed to torment the soul as much as the body.

Before I could process the horrific options further, the doctor's voice crackled menacingly through the PA system again. "Let me give you a clue. Do you want to keep your father or your friends Mike and Sarah?"

The starkness of the choice struck me like a physical blow. It was a monstrous decision to place upon anyone's shoulders, especially under such horrific circumstances. My mind raced, trying to decipher any hidden meanings or potential loopholes in his words, but the cold reality was clear: the doctor was forcing me to choose between the lives of my father and my closest friends.

I looked over at my father, his eyes sown shut. Then I thought of Mike and Sarah, loyal friends who had risked everything to help me, now potential pawns in this perverse game. The weight of the decision pressed down on me, suffocating and dark.

"Damn you! Why are you doing this?" I shouted into the void, hoping my voice would carry my fury and despair to the twisted mastermind behind this game.

The doctor's laugh echoed back; a sound devoid of any human warmth. "Because, my dear player, life is about making tough choices. And in this asylum, I am life."

I felt a surge of anger, but it was quickly drowned out by the necessity of the decision. "I need more time," I called out, stalling, hoping against hope for an opportunity to alter the course of the game.

"There is no more time," the doctor replied coolly. "Make your choice now, or I will choose for all of you."

The finality in his tone left no room for argument. I stood there, my mind frantically weighing each potential decision, each outcome more horrifying than the last. Choosing was a torment in itself, a mental torture that clawed at my sanity.

"Okay," I finally breathed out, my voice barely above a whisper. The word felt like a betrayal, a surrender to the darkness that the asylum embodied. But it was spoken, and with it, the die was cast.

I knew then that whatever happened next, my life and the lives of those I cared about were forever entwined with the shadows of the River Road Asylum. The game was set, the rules were cruel, and survival was far from guaranteed. The only certainty was the haunting reality that the choices made in this twisted game would indeed come back to haunt us, just as the doctor promised.

"Okay, I choose family you asshole. I choose family! Do you hear me!"

As Mike's voice filtered through the PA system, the betrayal stung sharply, a visceral punch that resonated with every fiber of my being. His words, light and taunting, clashed strangely with the oppressive atmosphere of the room. "Hey, my friend. I think you're going to have fun with your decision. I know you can't see me, but I'm waving on the other side of this two-way mirror."

My gaze shifted upwards, drawn by his words to the expansive mirror dominating the wall before me. The glass, cold and unyielding, reflected my battered image at me—a bleak reminder of the grim theatre in which I now played an unwilling part. This barrier, designed for silent observers to witness the gruesome unfold without staining their hands, now served as a chilling barrier between betrayer and betrayed.

With a mix of defiance and despair, I raised my right hand slowly, my fingers curling into a solitary, defiant gesture aimed at my unseen observers. I flipped off the mirror, a futile but satisfying act of rebellion against the twisted game I was ensnared in.

Laughter erupted from the speakers, Mike's voice returning, now laced with a cruel amusement. "Ouch, buddy. Don't be such a poor sport. This game is supposed to be fun." The lightness in his tone, so austerely at odds with the darkness of the dungeon-like room and the dire stakes of our grim reality, twisted the knife of betrayal deeper.

The incongruity of Mike's lighthearted banter filtering through the PA system, mixing creepily with the somber setting of the operating room. This chamber, shrouded in shadow and gleaming with the cold, indifferent sheen of surgical instruments, reeked of antiseptic—its biting, clinical scent mingling unnervingly with the cloying musk of Dr. Blackwell's cologne. Beneath these more dominant odors lingered the subtle, yet unmistakable, aroma of decay and dampness, an ever-present reminder of the room's morbid purposes.

The air felt thick, each breath a laborious effort, as if the oppressive atmosphere was trying to suffocate any semblance of hope. The glaring, artificial light from the overhead lamps cast severe shadows across the room, transforming the array of medical implements into sinister silhouettes—each one a potential instrument of agony. The walls, tiled and impersonal, seemed to close in, their surfaces chillingly reflective and unforgiving.

Amidst this chilling tableau, the sound of Mike's laughter resonating through the speakers struck a discordant note. It was a sound that, in any other context, might have been comforting or joyous. Yet here, it morphed into something sinister, a mockery of normalcy in an environment devoid of any true humanity. How could laughter, a sound so inherently filled with life and warmth, turn so cold and malevolent? It echoed off the hard, cold surfaces, an absurd reminder of the perversion of care and compassion that this place represented.

This dissonance left me disoriented and shaken, a frenzy of emotions swirling within. Confusion at the betrayal of a friend, fury at the casual cruelty, and an ever-deepening dread of what was yet to come combined into a suffocating fog of despair. The room, with its chilling precision and sterile surfaces, felt like a tableau vivant of my worst nightmares come to life, with the added horror of my impending ordeal all too real and imminent.

The chilling reality of my situation was inescapable. Trapped in this clinical hell, the juxtaposition of Mike's carefree mockery against the backdrop of looming surgical blades and the pervasive, musty stench of decay was not just jarring—it was a visceral assault, a brutal reminder of just how far I had fallen into the depths of this twisted game.

In this moment, trapped and tormented, the game Mike referred to was nothing short of a nightmare, its rules written by a madman and enforced by those I once called friends. The chilling reality that my pain was their entertainment was a bitter pill, one that filled me with a cold. Whatever Dr. Blackwell and Mike planned next, I knew my spirit, while battered, was not yet broken.

"Mike, why the fuck are you doing this? Mike?" My voice cracked as I called out, desperate for answers, for this to be some kind of sick joke.

My accusation was sharply interrupted by Dr. Blackwell's voice, which boomed through the PA system, his tone dripping with unsettling delight. "Oh, don't you worry, your friend Mike is perfectly safe—right here with me. He's proven quite cooperative, and exceedingly receptive to my guidance. In fact, he's become one of my most exemplary subjects."

The revelation hung heavy in the air; a brutal betrayal articulated with mocking pride. "You see, Mike has embraced a new role under my care," Dr. Blackwell continued his voice a sinister croon. "He's far more... compliant now, wonderfully modified to suit our needs here."

Then, with a sadistic cheerfulness, he added, "And now, let's focus on your current predicament, shall we? Notice the delicate stitching along both of your father's eyes. Somewhere behind those stitches lies the key to his restraints. You'll need to choose wisely and use the tools I've provided to retrieve it. Choose the correct eye, and you might just save him. But remember, we'll be keeping an eye on every cut you make—pun most definitely intended." His laugh was cold and mirthful, a chilling reminder of his control over not just my father's fate, but Mike's as well.

I turned toward my father, whose breathing had become ragged and uneven. His eyes once filled with a comforting warmth, now stared back at me, freakishly stitched shut. The reality of what I was being asked to do hit me like a wave of nausea. On the table beside me lay an array of sharp, gleaming tools—an assortment of scalpels, tweezers, and small clippers, each one gleaming under the harsh overhead lights.

Tears blurred my vision as I picked up a scalpel, its cold metal handle alien in my trembling hand. "I'm so sorry, Dad," I whispered, my voice choked with emotion. "I have no choice."

His muffled groans filled the air as I hesitated, the scalpel hovering over his right eye. Every fiber of my being revolted against the action I was about to take. But the haunting laughter over the PA reminded me of the stakes. With a deep, shuddering breath, I steadied my hand and began.

The first incision was ghastly. My hand trembled violently, the scalpel unfamiliar in my unsteady grip. I aimed for the stitches that crisscrossed the surgical site, intending only to cut through the thread. But my lack of skill and the shakiness of my hand betrayed me. The blade slipped, slicing deeper into the tender flesh beneath. The sound was horrific—wet and squelching, a visceral noise that resonated in the eerie silence of the room and reverberated in my skull, a stark reminder of the brutality of my actions.

Blood welled up from the gash, dark and thick, spilling over my fingers. It was warm and slick, coating my skin in a shiny glove that made the scalpel slip further. Each attempt to steady my hand failed more miserably than the last, my desperate sobs mingling with the chilling sound of my father's subdued groans. His body writhed weakly under the constraints, the muscles tensing in silent agony as the blade traced a crimson path across his skin.

Tears blurred my vision further, rendering the horrific tableau before me even more nightmarish. The dim light flickered above, mocking my faltering attempts. The key I was supposed to find—a small, benign piece of metal—was allegedly located behind one of his eyes. The thought of reaching for such a place with the scalpel was unbearable, a task so monstrous it threatened to fracture the last vestiges of my sanity.

With each passing second, the room seemed to close in around us, the walls whispering of death and desolation, echoing back the sickening sounds of flesh being parted. In this hellish moment, under the cold gaze of Dr. Blackwell, I was no longer a son trying to save his father; I was an unwilling participant in a dark ritual, forced to mutilate the one person I had sworn to protect. The morbid reality of my actions, driven by desperation and terror, was a weight too heavy to bear, a stain upon my soul that would never wash clean.

With trembling hands, I reached for the tweezers, inserting them delicately into the wound to feel around for the key. My stomach churned, bile rising in my throat as the metal clinked faintly against something hard. Carefully, I maneuvered the object, feeling its resistance against the soft tissues.

Finally, with a heart-wrenching tug, I extracted the small key, slick with blood and vitreous fluid. The sight of it, drenched in my father's suffering, was devastating. I hurriedly unlocked the cuffs, freeing his limp, trembling form from the table. His breathing was shallow and pained, but the worst was over. Or so I hoped.

As I wrapped my arms around him, supporting his weakened body, the doctor's voice returned, a sinister whisper through the PA. "Well done. But remember, the game isn't over yet. There are more choices to make, more games to play."

Every word sank deep, a grim cue that this nightmare was far from over. We were still pawns in the doctor's twisted game, with no clear path to salvation. As I steadied my father, promising silently to protect him from further harm, a tenacity like steel forged itself within me. Whatever it took, I would end this horror. The doctor would pay for what he had done, for turning a place of healing into a chamber of horrors.

I helped my father to a nearby chair, his body weak and trembling. Maybe it was all in my head but I swore I could smell the metallic tang of blood that lingered in the air, mixing with the antiseptic backdrop of the asylum. He was safe for the moment, but the doctor's voice crackled through the PA system once more, announcing the next horrific stage of his perverse game.

Hard Decision

"Now, let's move on to part two of our evening's entertainment," the doctor's voice oozed with malice. "Just like in the game of Life, you must decide your path forward—career or student. Choose wisely; each has its own... special outcomes."

The room chilled with his words, and I swallowed hard, my throat tight with fear. "What do you mean?" I called out, my voice echoing off the bare, unyielding walls of the operating room.

"Oh, it's quite simple," he replied, his voice tinged with a sadistic glee. "You can either train to become a doctor like myself, learning the ins and outs of my methods, or you can remain a student, observing the finer details of my work. But be warned, each choice comes with its own set of... experiences."

The choice was monstrous. Becoming a doctor under his tutelage meant participating in his grotesque procedures, violating every moral fiber I had left. Being a student meant witnessing unimaginable horrors, being forced to observe the mutilation and suffering of innocent victims—possibly including my friends—as part of some twisted educational regime.

I felt my stomach churn at the thought, the horror of either choice weighing heavily on me. I glanced at my father, his mutilated eyes meeting mine. He shook his head subtly, a silent plea not to succumb to the doctor's demands.

Gathering my courage, I responded with as much strength as I could muster. "I will not become a monster like you. I refuse to hurt anyone else."

The doctor's laughter boomed through the PA, chilling and mirthless. "Oh, you think you have a choice in becoming a monster? No, my dear guest, you misunderstood. The choice is merely about how you'll learn—actively or passively. You will learn either way."

When I refused to make the unbearable choice between becoming a tormentor or a passive witness to torment, Dr. Blackwell's laughter reverberated through the speaker with a sort of sadistic anticipation. "Very well, let the guards show you to your new quarters," he sneered, his voice laced with a chilling promise of retribution.

The air of the operating room was thick with the metallic tang of fresh blood and the underlying smell of old, musty, unwashed linens—a chilling backdrop to the horror that had just unfolded. My hand was still clutched around my father's, a desperate attempt to maintain some semblance of connection and protection, when the heavy door swung open with a jarring clang. Two of Dr. Blackwell's guards entered, their faces set in grim determination, eyes cold and unyielding.

As they approached, my heart pounded furiously, the echoes of my terror mingling with the labored breaths of my father beside me. Instinctively tightening my grip, I wrapped my other arm around my father's frail body, trying to shield him from the meager barrier of my form. His skin was clammy and cold under my embrace, but it was a contact that spoke of silent promises and unspoken apologies.

"Mike, if you can hear me, please do something! I know you're in there. Mike, please!

Mike, did not answer and all that met my screaming cries for help was the deafening sound of silence.

One guard, larger and more imposing, moved swiftly behind me. Before I could react, his arm was around my neck, locking me in a tight chokehold that immediately cut off my air supply. My lungs screamed for oxygen, and stars burst across my vision as panic set in. The second guard targeted my arm, his fingers finding the tender pressure point at my wrist with practiced ease. With a cruel twist, he forced my arm back at an unnatural angle, the pain sharp and blinding.

The agony was so intense that my grip faltered; my fingers uncurled against my will as I tried to focus on the pain rather than the fear of what was coming next. My father, disoriented and half-blind, reached out into the empty air where my hand had been. His stitched eye rendered him helpless, his vision marred by the blood that still oozed from my failed attempt to extract the key behind his other eye. He could only flail weakly, his fingers grasping nothing but the chilling emptiness.

His voice cracked as he attempted to call out my name, the sound heartbreaking in its desperation. The guards, unyielding and apparently indifferent to the human tragedy unfolding before them, dragged me away. My feet scraped helplessly against the cold floor, my body limp from the chokehold still tightly secured around my neck.

As I was pulled from the room, my father's distressing attempts to reach me filled the air, blending with the horrific sounds of the operating room. The last thing I heard as the door slammed shut was the muffled sound of his voice, strained and fading, drowned out by the distance and the thick, insulating walls of the asylum. The pain from the guard's manipulation of my arm, and the suffocating pressure around my neck, were consuming, but it was the sound of my father's helpless, disoriented cries that would haunt me, echoing in my ears long after I had been removed from his side.

With a vice-like grip, they dragged me from the clinical horror of the operating room. Their faces were impassive, their movements methodical, as if they were merely relocating an object rather than a person overwhelmed by fear and defiance. They hauled me down a series of decrepit hallways, the asylum's peeling paint and the stench of mold heavy in the air until we reached a remote section of the building.

They opened a heavy, metal door to reveal a small, padded room. The padding was aged and torn in places, revealing the hard, unforgiving walls beneath. This was to be my prison—a place designed to stifle screams and preserve secrecy.

"No! Let me go you fucking bastards. Let me go!"

Once inside, they left swiftly, the door slamming shut with an ominous clang that echoed off the padded walls. The room was desolate, save for a single speaker mounted high on one wall. Almost immediately, the tinny strains of "Sugar, Sugar" by the Archies began to play. At first, it seemed almost comical, the upbeat pop tune entirely at odds with the grim surroundings. But as the song looped again and again, each repetition became a thread in a tapestry of psychological torture.

The days began to merge, marked only by the relentless repetition of the song, which seeped into every crevice of my mind, its saccharine lyrics mocking me from above. The sensory deprivation of the padded room, combined with the incessant music, started to fray the edges of my sanity.

Food was slid through a small hatch at irregular intervals—plates of well-cooked meats that smelled tantalizingly rich. My initial resistance crumbled as hunger clawed at my stomach, driving me to consume the food with a desperate intensity. It was during one of these moments of weakness, as I savored the last bites of a particularly flavorful piece, that Dr. Blackwell's voice crackled through the PA system.

"I hope you enjoyed your meal," he said, his voice dripping with malicious satisfaction. "You've just savored a choice cut from your dear father. How does it feel to be so... intimately connected with your family?"

"You sick fuck! Please just let me out of here. I can't take it anymore!

His words were a psychological blow that struck with more force than any physical torture could have. I gagged, the remnants of the meal turning to ash in my mouth. Whether his claim was true or not, the seed of horror was planted. My mind reeled, teetering on the brink of madness as I grappled with the implications. Each subsequent meal became a psychological battleground, where the act of eating was tainted with revulsion and dread.

Trapped in that auditory hellscape, with only Dr. Blackwell's intermittent taunts for company, I felt the last vestiges of my determination beginning to crumble. The distinction between reality and the twisted fiction fed to me by the doctor blurred, leaving me to question everything, even my senses. The horror of not knowing—the fear that his words might be true—was perhaps the most torturous aspect of all.

"So, Ethan, are you ready to continue our family game night?" The doctor's voice boomed through the speaker.

"Fuck you, I'm not playing your twisted fucking game, asshole."

"I was hoping you wouldn't say that, Ethan. We can keep doing this for as long as you want. I have nothing but time on my hands."

"Just let us go. I promise we'll never speak of this place again." I said in a last-ditch effort to try to get out of this hell.

"Oh, my boy. It's far too late for that. Let's go ahead and move on to something new." Dr. Blackwell said and a sharp squeal screamed through the PA.

The void of silence that Dr. Blackwell imposed upon me was a cruel and unusual form of solitude. At first, the absence of "Sugar, Sugar" was a relief, a respite from the relentless assault on my senses. But soon, the silence itself became a thick, suffocating presence in the padded room, pressing in on me from all sides.

Days, or perhaps weeks—time had lost all meaning in this sensory deprivation chamber—began to blur into a single, continuous moment of isolation. The silence was so complete, so absolute, that my breaths seemed to roar in my ears, each inhale a raspy symphony, each exhale a desperate whisper of resistance.

"Is this better or worse?" I found myself speaking aloud, my voice sounding strange and distorted in the void. "Is silence better than that cursed song?" The sound of my voice was startling reminder of my solitude.

As the isolation deepened, my thoughts began to unspool, wandering freely without the anchor of external stimuli. Conversations with myself became my only solace, a way to fend off the creeping madness. "You know, this is just a game to him," I muttered, pacing the small confines of my room. "A twisted game, and you're just a pawn."

The shadows in the corners of the room seemed to shift and whisper in response, drawing my gaze with their subtle movements. "Are you real?" I challenged the darkness, half-expecting it to answer.

It was during one of these endless cycles of silence that she appeared—my mother, as vivid and real as any living person. "You're strong, stronger than he knows," she said, her voice clear and comforting in the oppressive silence.

"Mom?" My voice cracked the sound of it mingling with a sob. "How are you here? You're gone... you're not real."

She smiled gently, a sad tilt to her lips. "Maybe I'm not, but that doesn't mean I can't be here for you. You need to keep fighting, don't let him break you."

Talking to her, even knowing she was a figment of my fragmented psyche, became the highlight of my days. "I don't know if I can do this anymore, Mom. It's too much. The silence, it's eating at me," I confessed during one of her visits, my voice a low whisper, as if speaking too loudly might shatter the illusion of her presence.

"You can, and you will," she insisted. "Remember, strength isn't about enduring pain, it's about enduring the urge to give up. You have to keep going."

Our conversations, these dialogues with the apparition of my mother, grounded me in the ungrounded reality of my confinement. They provided a semblance of normalcy, a thread to hold onto in the unraveling tapestry of my mind.

Yet, even her spectral presence couldn't shield me entirely from the descent into madness. The padded walls began to feel like they were closing in, the space growing smaller with each passing day. I found myself speaking aloud more often, not just to her but to the room, to myself, to the silent observer I imagined Dr. Blackwell to be. "I won't let you win," I shouted, my voice hoarse with determination and despair. "You hear me, Blackwell? I'm not just a part of your sick game!"

The blend of isolation, hallucination, and self-dialogue swirled into a maelstrom of psychological turmoil, each element feeding off and fueling the others. As the boundary between reality and illusion blurred further, I clung to the echoes of my mother's words, a lifeline thrown across the dark waters of my mind, promising a shore I feared I might never reach.

As the days stretched endlessly onward, marked only by the timeless void of the filthy room, my mind began to teeter on the brink of complete madness. The silence, once a blessed relief, now clawed at the edges of my sanity, a suffocating blanket that muffled thoughts and warped perceptions. Within the confines of those four walls, devoid of any human contact, the lines between reality and hallucination began to blur irreparably.

It started subtly at first, a creeping sensation that my skin was becoming too tight for my body. This bizarre notion took root in the fertile ground of my isolation, growing more insistent with each passing hour. I would run my fingers along my arms, feeling the flesh that seemed to constrict with each beat of my heart. The texture felt foreign as if it were a suit I had outgrown but couldn't remove.

"Too tight," I murmured to myself, tugging at my forearm, my fingernails digging into the flesh. "It's all too tight." The walls echoed my words back to me, a twisted chorus that seemed to mock my growing distress.

One day, or perhaps it was night—the concept of time had long since lost all meaning—I sat huddled in a corner of the room, my fingers clawing at my skin. The sensation had become unbearable, a constant pressure that squeezed and suffocated. In a moment of horrific clarity, driven by the unrelenting belief that I needed to free myself from this constricting sheath, I began to scratch fervently.

Under my nails, the skin tore with a sickening ease, the sound oddly muffled by the padded walls. The pain was sharp, a searing contrast to the dull ache of the imagined constriction. Blood welled up from the small lacerations, warm and real against my cold, trembling fingers.

"This isn't right," I whispered hoarsely, pausing to inspect the damage. The sight of my blood, vibrant and undeniable on my hands, should have shocked me back to reality. Instead, it only fueled the madness, a visceral validation of my delusion.

I resumed my psychotic task with a manic fervor, peeling at the edges of the torn skin, convinced that beneath this suffocating layer lay relief. "I just need to get it off," I kept repeating, each word punctuated by the rip of tissue, the surreal soundscape of my undoing filling the room.

Hallucinations danced in the periphery of my vision, shadows morphing into demonic spectators who watched with glee. My mother's apparition appeared again, her face twisted in horror and sorrow. "Stop, please, stop!" she pleaded, her voice a ghostly whisper that struggled to rise above the frenzy.

But her pleas fell on deaf ears, drowned out by the roar of my desperation. The pain, the blood, the tearing—it all blended into a nightmarish symphony that drowned out any semblance of reason.

I don't know how long I continued, lost in that hellish loop of self-mutilation. It was only when the door finally swung open, revealing the silhouettes of Dr. Blackwell and his guards, that some semblance of awareness crept back into my fogged mind. They advanced, their expressions a mix of disgust and cold fascination.

Dr. Blackwell's voice cut through the chaos, clinical and detached. "It seems our subject has taken a rather... personal approach to his studies." The guards restrained me once more, pulling me away from the bloodstained corner, my hands and arms raw and exposed, the horrific evidence of my breakdown blatant against the sterile white of their gloves.

The Caring Doctor

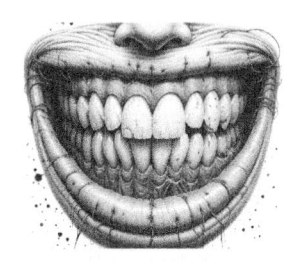

As they dragged me back towards the realm of the doctor's twisted care, the reality of what I had done began to sink in, a crushing weight that threatened to pull me under into the dark abyss of total madness.

As Dr. Blackwell and the guards escorted me through the labyrinthine corridors of the asylum, my mind reeled from the damage I had done to myself. The unembellished contrast between my mutilated arms and the doctor's clinical detachment added an extra layer of surrealism to the nightmare I was living. We stopped in front of a door that looked remarkably mundane compared to the rest of the facility's foreboding architecture.

The door swung open to reveal an interior glaringly contrasted with the grim decay of the rest of the asylum. The room was bright and airy, decorated in the style of a typical doctor's office, complete with polished wooden furniture and neatly framed posters on the walls. One poster featured a cartoon cat dangling from a branch, accompanied by the optimistic phrase "Hang in there," its cheerfulness almost mocking in context.

Dr. Blackwell's demeanor had undergone a transformation as profound as the room's decor. His voice, previously tinged with sadistic glee, was now soothing and fatherly. "Now, why would you go and do that to yourself?" he asked, tsk-tsking as he guided me to a plush examination chair that seemed out of place with its gleaming chrome and soft leather.

I was too dazed and in shock to respond, my eyes fixating on the incongruously cheerful poster as Dr. Blackwell began to tend to my wounds. His movements were gentle and precise, a stark contradiction to the cruel manipulator who had orchestrated so much suffering. As he cleaned each wound with expert care, the sting of antiseptic on raw skin brought a sharp clarity back to my foggy mind.

"But don't worry, we'll get you all fixed up," he continued, smiling warmly as he applied bandages with practiced ease. His smile, meant to be reassuring, only deepened the eerie sense of dissonance I felt. Here was the man who had tormented me, now playing the role of a benevolent healer.

"Fixed up for what?" I finally managed to croak, my voice hoarse from disuse and emotional strain.

Dr. Blackwell paused, his hands still for a moment as he looked directly into my eyes. "For a fresh start, of course. We all deserve a chance to erase our mistakes and begin anew, don't we?" His tone was almost convincing as if he truly believed in the possibility of redemption he was suggesting.

I glanced again at the poster, the cat hanging on determinedly. It felt like a cruel joke, a reminder of the persistence required to endure this place. "Hang in there," indeed—as if survival were just a matter of enduring a little longer, a little stronger.

As Dr. Blackwell finished bandaging my arms, he stepped back, admiring his handiwork. "There, much better," he declared, his voice brimming with satisfaction. "We'll keep a close eye on you, and ensure you're healing nicely, both physically and mentally."

He didn't need to say it outright, but I understood the subtext clearly: my compliance was expected, and my recovery was framed as another step in his twisted game. The room, with its deceptive normalcy, was just another arena for his psychological manipulations. Whether I was to be a doctor or a patient in his eyes, the role I was expected to play was clear. Yet, beneath his care, the silent storm within me stirred, a quiet determination to resist, to survive, not just to "hang in there" but to somehow, someday, break f ree.

The room seemed to be alive, its walls pulsating with the beat of my heart as Dr. Blackwell posed his insidious question, his voice silky smooth, laced with faux concern that didn't quite reach his eyes. The smell of the doctor's nasty Old Spice cologne was heavy in the air, mingling with the faint aroma of polished wood from the furniture, creating a facade of normalcy that was as disconcerting as the situation itself.

"So, are we ready to make a decision yet?" His tone was gentle, almost coaxing, as if he were discussing something as mundane as choosing a dinner menu, not deciding the fate of my sanity.

I looked up at him, his features obscured behind the perpetual smiley face mask, an eerie and constant reminder of his detachment from the horrors he inflicted. The mask seemed to grin down at me, its cheer a blatant mockery of my plight. My eyes then dropped to the floor, the polished tiles reflecting the fluorescent lights above, each gleam a flicker of the turmoil I felt inside.

I was caught in a tormenting dilemma—agreeing to his terms felt like surrendering a part of my soul, yet the thought of returning to the padded room, with its oppressive silence and maddening isolation, filled me with an even greater dread. The memories of my skin feeling too tight, of tearing at my flesh in a desperate attempt to escape an invisible prison, were too fresh, too raw.

The doctor placed a hand on my shoulder, the contact startling me. "Listen here, son," he began, his voice dripping with a paternalistic tone that belied the cruelty of his actions. "I don't like what we are doing any more than you do. But you need to understand that this is all part of the process. If you don't think you are ready, then we continue our work on you for as long as it takes. Remember, I'm only trying to help you."

His words, meant to reassure, felt like a velvet glove over an iron fist—a soft touch masking a threatening presence. The pressure of his hand was a physical reminder of his control, both immediate and omnipresent.

I took a deep breath, the cool air of the room filling my lungs, mingling with the scent of leather from the chair beneath me. The decision lay heavy on my chest, a burden I felt in every fiber of my being. I knew in my heart that Dr. Blackwell enjoyed this manipulation, this game of cat and mouse, yet I also knew I couldn't endure much more.

With a heavy heart, I lifted my head, meeting the gaze of the smiling mask. "I'll... I'll continue," I muttered, each word tasting like defeat. The mask seemed to smile wider, if such a thing were possible, as if pleased with my capitulation.

"Very good," Dr. Blackwell replied, his voice smooth as honey, yet cold as ice. "I knew you'd make the right choice. So, what's it going to be, career or student?"

"Student, sir. I guess I choose a student."

"Ah, the path of the observer," the doctor mused. "Very well. Prepare yourself for a lesson in human anatomy like no other."

As he removed his hand from my shoulder and stepped back, signaling to the guards who had lingered silently by the door, a part of me felt like I had just signed away more than I could ever comprehend. Yet another part, a smaller, quieter part, clung to a sliver of hope—hope that playing along might eventually lead to some opportunity, some way to escape the nightmare that the River Road Asylum had become.

The guards approached, their movements efficient and devoid of any emotion, as I was led away from the mock doctor's office and deeper into the bowels of the asylum. Each step was a step further into the unknown, each moment a moment closer to discovering what "preparation" meant in the twisted world of Dr. Blackwell.

We walked through a series of chillingly sterile corridors, the screams and cries of patients growing louder as we approached an operating theater. The room was set up like a classroom, with tiered seating, all facing a central surgical table illuminated by bright, harsh lights.

The Student

There, strapped to the table, was another patient, their eyes wide with terror. The doctor, already dressed in surgical garb, waved me over with a sinister smile. "Come, observe closely. You'll learn what happens when the human body is no longer seen as a vessel for the soul but as a canvas for medical exploration."

As I took my place in the front row, the room's cold sterility contrasted sharply with the warmth of the blood that I knew would soon be spilled. Every tool, every monitor hummed with the promise of forthcoming horror. I realized then that my role as a student was not just to watch but to witness and remember, to carry the truth of these atrocities beyond these walls—somehow, someday.

In the dimly lit operating theater, the air was thick as a cold chill seeped into my bones, carrying with it a sense of impending dread. The stark white lights above the surgical table cast an unforgiving glow on the patient strapped down before me, their skin pale and stretched tight with terror. The doctor, clad in his pristine surgical gown, loomed over them like a psychotic artist ready to begin his cadaverous masterpiece.

I felt a strong urge to shut my eyes, to block out the horror that I knew was about to unfold. But before I could retreat into the darkness behind my eyelids, rough hands grabbed me. One guard held me firmly by the shoulders, pinning me to the aged oak seating of the amphitheater, while another approached with a small, menacing device in hand. It was a pair of wire speculums, and with a clinical indifference, he fitted them onto my eyes, forcing my eyelids wide open. The cold metal bit into my flesh, a cruel reminder that there would be no averting my gaze. My hands were then secured tightly to the arms of the chair with hemp ropes, the fibers chafing against my wrists.

Bound and immobilized, I was made a captive audience to the doctor's gruesome performance. He approached the patient with a chilling calmness, selecting his instruments with deliberate care from a tray that gleamed with an array of polished steel. Each tool was laid out meticulously—a scalpel, a pair of forceps, a serrated bone saw—all instruments of torture masquerading as surgical implements.

Dr. Blackwell approached the gleaming tray of instruments with a showman's flair, each movement calculated to draw maximum suspense. As I sat immobilized, my heart pounding in dread, he lifted each tool, presenting them with a twisted enthusiasm.

"Ah, let's introduce our cast of characters, shall we?" he began, his voice tinged with a morbid gaiety. Picking up the scalpel, he held it delicately between his fingers, turning it this way and that, allowing the overhead lights to catch the polished steel. "This here is the scalpel—sharp, precise, unforgiving. It makes the first incision, slicing through the skin as easily as a hot knife through butter. The beauty of this tool lies in its simplicity and the clean lines it carves in the flesh. A true artist's brush!"

Setting down the scalpel, he reached for the bone saw, his grin widening. "Now, this fellow is quite different," he chuckled, hefting the serrated tool with an exaggerated flourish. "The bone saw—a bit more brute force required here. It's perfect for those tough, gnarly bits like ribs and femurs. You'll hear its song soon—a gritty, grinding symphony that cuts through the silence of this grand theater."

Next came the forceps, which he waved almost comically in the air. "These are not your ordinary tweezers. Forceps! Ideal for plucking out those troublesome little pieces that like to hide away. Clamps, grips, retrieves—oh, the fun we can have with these! Like playing a game of operation, only the stakes are oh-so deliciously high."

He paused, his eyes catching mine, ensuring I was watching every disgusting detail. "And we mustn't forget the gauze pads," he added, picking up a stack with a flourish. "Not nearly as thrilling as the others, but every artist needs a good eraser to clear away the excess—blood, fluids, the little messes that arise. Cleanliness is next to godliness, right?"

Each instrument was introduced with a perverse pride, Dr. Blackwell reveling in the horrified fascination he saw flicker across my face. He laid them out like a twisted collection, his descriptions painting vivid images of the pain they could inflict.

Finally, he picked up a large needle with an attached syringe, his expression turning momentarily serious. "And last but certainly not least, the anesthetic—because we're not barbarians, are we? We must ensure our guest is comfortable, if not entirely... cooperative." His laugh, following this statement, was hollow and echoing, bouncing off the not-so-sterile walls and filling the room with its menace.

"Ready to begin, are we?" Dr. Blackwell asked rhetorically, his dark eyes glinting with a madness that seemed to deepen with the shadows of the looming surgery. "Let's proceed with the show—after all, we wouldn't want our audience to grow bored."

Each word dripped with distorted humor, his enthusiasm for the suffering he was about to inflict making the chilling tableau all the more terrifying. The instruments lay neatly arrayed, each one an actor in the ghastly drama about to unfold, with Dr. Blackwell as the unhinged conductor of a symphony of screams.

The doctor began with the scalpel, its sharp blade catching the harsh light as he made an incision with surgical precision along the patient's abdomen. The skin parted under the blade, revealing a hint of the visceral horror beneath. The patient's muffled screams filled the room, a sound hushed by the gag that cruelly silenced their agony. Blood welled up from the incision, a vivid crimson that contrasted harshly against the pallid flesh.

With a perverse meticulousness, the doctor placed his hands into the open wound, his gloves stained with blood as he explored the cavity. His movements were unhurried, almost reverent, as he narrated his actions for his forced pupil's 'educational benefit'. "Observe the elasticity of the abdominal fascia," he said, his voice eerily composed as he manipulated the exposed tissues with his forceps, lifting them for me to see.

The room echoed with the subtle clinks of metal on metal and the wet sounds of flesh being manipulated and dissected. Despite the speculums forcing my eyes open, my vision began to blur with involuntary tears, each drop a silent testament to the horror I was powerless to stop.

As the doctor continued his grim demonstration, moving from organ to organ with a twisted curiosity, the patient's muffled cries grew weaker, their body trembling under the relentless assault. The doctor's hands were unyielding, his fascination with his work apparent in his meticulous focus and the disturbing enthusiasm in his voice. "Now, let's examine the strength of the human skeletal structure," he announced, reaching for the serrated bone saw
.

The sound of the saw's teeth grinding against bone was nightmarish, a cacophony that echoed monstrously in the confined space of the theater. The patient convulsed, the straps holding them down creaking under the strain of their agony.

Each moment stretched into an eternity of torment, a vivid tableau of human cruelty that imprinted itself indelibly on my mind. Bound to my chair, forced to watch the unspeakable, I realized that my spirit was being dissected, the very essence of my humanity challenged and mutilated by the spectacle of brutality before me. This was no education; it was an indoctrination into darkness, a lesson in the depths to which human depravity could sink.

As the bizarre concerto of flesh and steel played out before me, a desperate, burgeoning notion of escape began to take root in my mind. While the doctor was engrossed in his seemingly exhilarating work, his focus entirely on his grisly demonstration, I noticed a slight give in the ropes that bound my wrists to the chair. The bindings, while tight, were not as secure as the guards had intended, a small oversight in their confidence in the physical restraints.

Heart pounding with a mix of fear and adrenaline, I began to subtly work my wrists back and forth, twisting them in small, cautious movements. The rope, coarse and unyielding, bit into my skin with each twist, the friction burning and raw. I winced in pain as the fibers scraped against my skin, the sensation sharp and intense. The motion was slow, excruciatingly so, but with each painstaking rotation, I could feel the rope loosening ever so slightly.

Determined, I continued, ignoring the searing pain that soon turned into a warm trickle of blood. My wrists began to bleed, the ropes now slick with my blood, which ironically aided my efforts. The lubrication of the blood allowed me to maneuver my hands with more ease, the ropes slipping against the wetness. I grimaced as the sharp pain mixed with a nauseous relief, aware that my window of opportunity was narrow and fraught with risk.

As the doctor's back was turned, his attention fully captured by his surgical exploration, I managed to twist one hand free. The relief was immediate, but there was no time to savor it. Quickly, I worked on the other wrist, the rope was now even more cooperative with the assistance of the blood acting as a lubricant.

Finally free, my hands trembled both from the strain and the surge of adrenaline that coursed through my veins. I carefully removed the wire speculums and glanced around quickly, assessing my situation. The doctor was still absorbed in his task, the body of his patient laid open like an ill-shaped book, his commentary to himself filled with a chilling enthusiasm. The guards were positioned by the door, their attention fixed casually on the doctor's work, confident in the security measures they had placed upon me.

Carefully, I eased myself out of the chair, my movements slow and deliberate to avoid any sudden noises. My feet touched the cold floor, and I paused, holding my breath, listening for any sign that my actions had been noticed. The room continued to echo with the dark and disgusting sounds of the operation, covering the soft sound of my movements.

Stealthily, I moved away from the chair, keeping my eyes on the doctor and the guards. I needed to find a way out, to navigate through the maze of corridors and find a route to freedom. Every step was fraught with peril, the stakes... life and death. I knew I couldn't leave without trying to save my father, my friends, and possibly others trapped in this nightmare.

The door to the operating theater seemed miles away, but I forced myself to focus, to move with purpose while every sense was alert to the smallest change in the room's dynamics. The escape plan was desperate and risky, but it was a chance—a chance to end this nightmare, a chance for survival. The only advantage I had was the cold darkness surrounding the well-lit operating table. If I could somehow make it to the door while the guards were enthralled in the work of Dr. Blackwell, I may have a chance.

As I edged closer to the door, every nerve in my body screaming for escape, the doctor's abrupt movement caught my peripheral vision. He walked over to the plexiglass barrier that enclosed the operating area and slammed his bloodied hands onto it, the impact sending a jarring crack through the silent tension. I froze, my heart pounding, as I turned to see him staring directly at me. His gaze was intense, his eyes almost gleaming with a disturbing delight.

"Where do you think you're going?" he called out, his voice eerily calm yet filled with a menacing undertone. "I think you're going to want to stick around for our next patient. Trust me, you're going to want to see this." His laugh, hollow and chilling, echoed through the room, his blood-stained hands leaving a smeared, crimson print on the plexiglass.

"Guards, bring out patient number two," he commanded with a wave of his hand. As he uncuffed the first patient from the table and rolled him off, the man's body made a loud, disturbing thud against the hard linoleum floor. The sound of his fall was a clear recollection of the reality of the situation.

My breath caught sharply as the guards ushered in another figure, a hauntingly familiar form that took my breath away. Realization struck like a hammer, and dread pooled cold in my stomach. "No, please... don't hurt him," I pleaded, my voice cracking under the weight of my terror. "Dad, I'm so sorry."

Dr. Blackwell's laughter filled the room, laced with a disturbing glee. "Oh, Ethan, you're really going to enjoy what we've planned for dear old dad here." His voice was buoyant with sick excitement.

"You sick fuck, let him go!" I shouted, raw emotion tearing through my words.

Dr. Blackwell waved dismissively at me, a twisted smirk in his tone. "Ethan, do take a seat. Your outbursts are upsetting our patient," he chided as if we were merely spectators in a twisted game of his design.

Fixing Dad

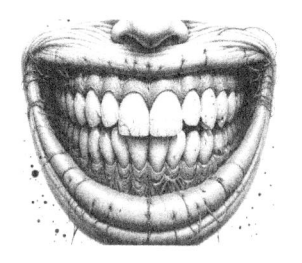

The doctor chuckled darkly. "Ethan, your dad has always been an angry man. I'm going to fix that for you. He will be much more pleasant to be around once I'm finished." The casualness with which he spoke about altering my father's very essence sent waves of horror through me.

My dad struggled against the guards' grip as they rolled him onto the table and secured his arms, legs, and head. His closed eyes met mine, and though terribly disfigured I could tell were filled with fear and defiance, a silent plea for help that I felt powerless to answer.

I charged up to the plexiglass, my fists pounding against it in a frenzy of desperation.

"Dammit, Ethan!" Dr. Blackwell's voice cut through the chaos, sharp and commanding. He quickly smoothed over his initial outburst, his tone becoming unnervingly calm. "Sorry about that, Ethan. Please, step back so I can focus. Any misstep here, and you may never see your father again."

Reluctantly, I stepped back, my pleas becoming increasingly frantic yet seemingly unheard. My words seemed to dissipate into the sterile air, powerless against the cold barrier between us.

Dr. Blackwell turned away from me, his attention focusing back on the chilling array of surgical instruments laid out before him. "Now, where were we," he mused aloud, his voice chillingly casual as he resumed his grim work, "before we were so rudely interrupted."

The doctor then picked up a sinister-looking tool from his tray. Holding it up, almost as if he were showing off a prized possession, he announced, "This here is called a Leucotome. You see, the lobotomy hasn't been performed in a few years due to all the weak-minded fools who think they know better. Well, I'm bringing it back." The gleam in his eye was one of madness mixed with a disturbing sense of purpose.

He positioned himself at the head of the table, aligning the Leucotome with the same eye where I had found the handcuff key earlier. My father's muffled cries of protest were heart-wrenching, but they did nothing to deter the doctor. With a practiced motion, he inserted the ice pick-like tool through the corner of my father's eye socket.

The procedure was overwhelming. The sound of the Leucotome piercing through soft tissue, the sight of my father's body tensing up in agony—it was a brutality that transcended the physical. It was a violation of his very being, an erasure of the man he was.

Tears streamed down my face, hot and unyielding, as I watched helplessly. The doctor worked with horrifying precision, twisting the tool with mechanical efficiency. When he finally pulled the Leucotome out, the damage was done. My father's body relaxed suddenly, a sign of the profound alteration the doctor had inflicted on his brain.

As the doctor stepped back, admiring his work with sick satisfaction, I knew I had witnessed one of the most barbaric acts in medical history.

The ominous flicker of the overhead lights cast ghastly shadows across the room as the doctor reveled in the setup for the next phase of his diabolical game. His chilling voice, a whisper laden with malice, reverberated through clinical chamber, making the air itself feel heavier, more suffocating.

Great Escape

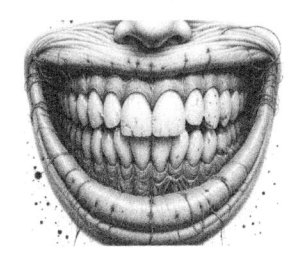

"For this next part," he intoned, his eyes gleaming with perverse anticipation, "you will have the pleasure of choosing between two 'Life' cards. Each card orchestrates a different fun little scenario. Unfortunately for you, neither choice will bring anything but gleeful agony."

He opened a small, ornate box, its surface embellished with disturbingly intricate carvings of human suffering. From it, he drew two aged, yellowed cards, their corners curled and edges frayed as if they had been handled by countless doomed players before me.

"Card one," he announced, holding up the first card between his blood-stained fingers, "will grant you the opportunity for a unique sacrifice. This choice involves a little experiment to 'enhance' your sensory perception. We'll surgically modify your auditory nerves to see just how acute your hearing can get. Imagine hearing everything, even the faintest whisper of death in the walls of this place."

The suggestion sent a visceral shiver down my spine, the thought of my body being mutilated to amplify every scream and sob within these cursed walls was horrifying.

He allowed the dread to simmer before he flipped to the second card, his voice dripping with dark delight. "Card two offers a test of your physical limits. How long can one endure the relentless surge of electricity through their body? It's a shocking ordeal, designed to push you to the very brink of your endurance—and perhaps beyond."

Each choice was crafted to torment, to break spirit and flesh alike. The doctor's twisted game was a ludicrous mockery of life's unpredictability, transforming the innocuous twists of fate into a nightmare of cruel and unusual punishments.

As he shuffled the cards with an unsettling carelessness, the soft rustling sound felt like a prelude to imminent horror. "Make your choice," he urged, a sinister smile playing on his lips, hidden beneath the mask. "And remember, while life is about the journey, in this game, it's the horrific detours that count."

My heart pounded as I weighed my grim options. Choosing between sensory mutilation and physical torture was like deciding which dark path to take in a labyrinth designed by a madman. Both led to suffering, both promised a journey through unimaginable horrors.

Resigned to my fate yet determined to survive, I reached out with a trembling hand, the cold dread pooling in my stomach. The game was rigged, the choices a mere illusion of control. But my resolve to find a way out, to save myself and my father, hardened within me like forged steel.

"Card two," I whispered, barely audible, choosing the path of endurance over permanent mutilation. As I declared my choice, the room seemed to close in around me, the air thick with the electric anticipation of the horrors to come. The doctor nodded; his satisfaction apparent as he prepared the instruments of torture.

As the guards approached to strap me into the contraption designed for this cruel test, my mind raced with plans of escape, every nerve screaming for freedom. This wasn't just a battle for survival—it was a war against the darkest depths of human depravity, and I was right at its heart.

Everything within me screamed to fight, to flee, to do whatever it took to avoid the fate that the doctor had laid out before me. As they grabbed my arms to strap me in, I twisted violently, catching one guard off-guard with an elbow to the ribs. He stumbled back, his grip loosening just enough for me to break free.

My heart raced as adrenaline surged through my veins. I lunged for the surgical tray, my hand closing around the cold handle of a scalpel. With a desperate swing, I drove the sharp blade into the side of the doctor's face as he moved to intercept me. The scalpel sank deep, and his reaction was not of pain but a burst of horrific, maniacal laughter. He touched the handle of the scalpel, his eyes locked on mine, and then, with a chilling smile, he yanked it out, blood streaming down the mask on his face in a repulsive cascade.

Seizing the moment of his distraction, I turned and sprinted from the operating room. The sound of my footsteps echoed through the bleak corridors; the shouts of the guards close behind me. Fear propelled me forward, a wild, frantic energy that sharpened my senses. I needed a hiding place, needed to think, needed to plan—not just my escape, but how to rescue my father and hopefully my friends from this nightmare.

I darted down a hallway lined with doors, each likely leading to rooms as horrific as the one I had just fled. My breath was loud in my ears, a harsh reminder of the perilously thin line between captivity and freedom I was navigating. Finally, spotting a slightly ajar door leading to what appeared to be a supply closet, I slipped inside and quietly clicked it shut behind me.

Inside, the dimly lit room was cramped and filled with shelves stocked with linens and medical supplies. I pressed myself against the cool wall, trying to control my breathing as I listened to the guards' footsteps thundering past. The momentary safety was suffocating, the silence a bleak contrast to the chaos of just minutes before.

As I waited for the distant sounds of pursuit to fade, my mind raced with plans. I had to find my father before they regrouped and intensified their search. I knew that every second counted and that the doctor would be furious and even more dangerous now.

Emerging from the supply closet, the dimly lit corridor stretched ominously before me. The eerie quiet was suddenly shattered by the crackle of the PA system, and a voice that echoed through the stale air of the asylum. It was a familiar voice, one that filled me with a mix of dread and confusion.

"Son, let the doctor help you like he helped me. Son, let the doctor help you as he helped me," the voice repeated mechanically, almost as if it were stuck on a loop, its tone hauntingly calm and unnervingly steady.

Just as the voice was about to repeat the phrase, an abrupt interruption came over the PA, the doctor's voice dripping with irritation and mockery. "Shut up! We get it. Let the doctor help you like he helped me," he mimicked in a whiny, high-pitched voice that contrasted sharply with the somber repetition of the earlier message. "I think he gets the picture."

There was a brief pause, the silence hanging heavily in the air, before the doctor continued, his tone shifting to one of taunting nonchalance. "Listen, Ethan, the front door is wide open. All you have to do is leave."

The offer, delivered so casually, hung in the air like a trap waiting to be sprung. The simplicity of the choice laid before me—to simply walk out and abandon the nightmarish game, leaving behind my father, friends, and the unresolved horrors of the asylum—was both a temptation and a torment.

As I stood there, processing the implications, the weight of my decision pressed heavily on my shoulders. The doctor's offer to just walk away was seductive, promising an easy end to the terror. But it was laced with the bitter knowledge that leaving would mean leaving my father and dear friends behind, subject to whatever "help" the doctor had subjected him to, the kind of help that turned a loving father into a voice on the PA system, parroting madness.

Drawing a deep breath, I steadied myself. The doctor's games, his twisted treatments, had changed the ones I held dear, perhaps irrevocably. But I couldn't leave them in this place, a pawn in the doctor's cruel experiments. The decision was harrowing but clear. I had to stay. I had to end this, not just escape it.

"No," I said aloud, though no one but the shadows could hear me. "I'm not leaving without them. I'm finishing this."

With determination fueling my steps, I moved away from the direction of the supposed escape, heading deeper into the heart of the asylum. Each step was a defiance, a declaration that I wouldn't be swayed by the lure of an easy out. There were things more important than my safety, and I was prepared to face whatever horrors awaited to bring my father back, to bring my friends back, to truly finish the game on my terms, not the doctors.

Finishing The Game

The corridors of the asylum twisted and turned like the innards of some great beast, each hallway darker and more foreboding than the last. The echo of my father's voice looped hauntingly through the air, a broken record that seemed to seep out from the very walls: "Son, let the doctor help you as he helped me." The words, repeated with eerie consistency, were both a beacon and a torment, drawing me deeper into the labyrinthine depths.

Following the sound, I stumbled upon a padded room, the door ajar with a soft, yellow light spilling out onto the darkened floor. Inside, the scene was one of chilling resignation. My father sat in the center of the room, chains binding him to the cold concrete beneath him. Strangely, he seemed at peace, an unsettling calmness to his demeanor that belied the cruel reality of his bondage.

As I stepped into the room, my heart pounding with a mix of relief and dread, a shadow moved from the corner—an unseen assailant who had waited for my arrival.

Before I could react, a sharp pain pierced my neck, a needle driving deep and injecting its disturbing contents into my bloodstream. The room spun wildly, and darkness clawed at the edges of my vision, pulling me down into unconsciousness.

When I awoke, the world came back in a haze of pain and confusion. My face felt like it was engulfed in flames, a searing agony that made it difficult to even think. Struggling to my feet, I staggered to a nearby grimy window, the reflection revealing the horror of my new reality. My face had been hideously altered, carved into a permanent, monstrous smile—mimicking the fate that had befallen Sarah. Nausea churned in my stomach as my fingers on one hand, wrapped in surgical gauze, trembled as they touched the jagged edges of my mutilated lips.

The PA system crackled to life once more, the doctor's voice oozing through with a malicious glee. "Well, since you're having a hard time playing by the rules, I have come up with a punishment. And if you make it through this, you and your father can leave. I give you, my word. While you were sleeping like a baby, I took the liberty of removing your fingers. Yup, all five from one hand. See I'm a nice guy, I left you with one good hand, and they are hidden throughout the hospital. If you can find them all before my favorite song ends, then you are free to go. Please act quickly."

The horror of his words settled in, a sickening twist to his already demented game. Not only had he mutilated my face, but he had also amputated my fingers, turning them into morbid tokens in a gruesome treasure hunt.

Each word from the PA system echoed in my ears, a taunt that filled me with both horror and an indomitable will to survive.

Gritting my teeth against the pain, I made a silent vow. I would find my fingers, save my father, and escape this nightmare. The stakes were unimaginable, but so too was my testicular fortitude. With each painful step, I began the grisly search through the dark corridors, the doctor's laughter still echoing behind me, a chilling reminder of the game's high stakes.

The crackle of the PA system halted my steps. The doctor's voice, thick with malicious glee, echoed through the gloomy corridors of the asylum, setting the stage for the next phase of his twisted game.

"I'll give you a clue before you start your little scavenger hunt," the doctor taunted over the PA. "I fed five patients with a sammie, each with one phalange. You may have to do some surgery, so I hope you paid attention in class. The doors are marked so the awaiting patients should not be too hard to find." His boisterous laughter faded into a sinister silence that seemed to wrap itself around the cold walls. Then the deafening sound of music came through the speakers. I knew this song, it had just come out on record and was one of my favorite bands. "I can't believe I'm doing this to the soundtrack of Whipping Post by The Allman Brothers Band. This better be the live version or I don't have much time."

Armed with this grim information, I left the safety of the room, my will be steeled by the urgency of finding the five fingers he had cruelly hidden—pieces of myself that I needed to reclaim. The daunting reality of what lay ahead pressed heavily upon me as I navigated the dimly lit hallways. Each step brought me closer to the other patients who unknowingly carried parts of me within them, heightening the gravity of my mission.

"Okay, room number one. This has to be it." I said silently to myself.

Approaching the first room, I hesitated at the door, the sounds of shallow breathing escaping from within. Strengthening my nerves, I entered, finding a patient lying motionless, their chest rising and falling rhythmically. The stark overhead light cast unembellished shadows across their form, making the room feel even more like a tableau of dread.

Beside the patient lay a scalpel, and with a heavy heart, I picked it up, its handle cold and impersonal in my grip. "I'm so sorry," I murmured, more to steady my resolve than anything else. Carefully, I made an incision, the clinical detachment I strove for barely holding at bay the nausea and horror swirling within me. My hands, though steady, felt alien as they moved with practiced precision.

Inside the stomach, amidst this poor patient's entrails, I found the first finger. It was a surreal and horrifying moment, each discovery a grotesque confirmation of the doctor's madness.

As I ventured from one ghastly room to the next, the sadistic ritual became a horrifying monotony, each space a sickening reflection of the last. Every patient I encountered was ensnared in the doctor's sick game, their bodies unwitting vessels harboring fragments of my very being.

The unadorned, clinical rooms, bathed in the harsh light of necessity, became stages for a grim ballet of recovery and despair. With each incision I made, a piece of me was reclaimed, yet something deeper and more intangible was lost.

The corridors of the asylum seemed to stretch and contort with each passing moment, the walls themselves whispering of anguish and madness. By the time I extracted the fifth and final finger, the dim glow of predawn light had begun to filter through the barred windows, casting eerie, elongated shadows that danced across the cold, concrete floors. The light, pale and unyielding, seemed almost accusatory, illuminating the gruesome reality of my quest.

As the last haunting notes of a distant, forgotten song played somewhere within the depths of the asylum, echoing like a lament through the hollow halls, I realized I had finished just in time. My voice, ragged and hoarse, broke the oppressive silence that followed. "I did it, you son of a bitch, I did it. Now let me go." My words were a defiant proclamation, my bloodied hands raised high in a gesture that felt both triumphant and tragic.

But the only response was the continued wails and cries of the unseen, their voices a vivid recollection of the ongoing torment surrounding me. My supposed victory felt hollow, the weight of my actions heavy upon my shoulders. The bleak reality settled around me like a shroud; though I had reclaimed my missing fingers, I was still ensnared in a nightmare of the doctor's making.

I stood there, in the dim light of dawn, surrounded by the echo of my desperate affirmation, waiting for a freedom that felt as distant as the fading darkness outside. As I awaited the doctor's next move, the oppressive atmosphere of the asylum seemed to tighten around me, a tangible reminder that the game might change its rules but never its nature. Exhausted, physically and emotionally, I clutched the fingers wrapped in a piece of cloth, their significance far greater than the sum of their parts. They were not just lost pieces of myself but symbols of the resilience and horror I had endured.

Dr. Blackwell's voice came through the PA, smooth and unsettlingly cordial. "As promised, I'm a man of my word, Ethan. I must admit, you've impressed me. Your father is waiting for you just outside in the hallway. However, your friends Sarah and Mike will be remaining under my care for the time being. Sarah isn't in a condition to look after herself, and Mike has graciously agreed to stay on and assist with some... essential duties."

Heart pounding, I hurried into the hallway. There, to my immense relief, was my father, looking bewildered but unharmed. I rushed to him, wrapping him in a fierce, protective hug, the contact grounding me in the reality that he was safe, at least for now.

As I held him, I turned back towards the room, my voice resolute and filled with a cold fury. "I'll be back for my friends, you asshole," I promised, my words slicing through the sterile air of the asylum.

Dr. Blackwell's laughter echoed faintly in response, a sinister sound that seemed to follow me as I led my father away from the dark heart of the asylum. The dawn was breaking, casting long shadows that retreated like the remnants of a bad dream. Yet, the promise I had made lingered, a vow etched deep in my heart, propelled by a determination to return and end the nightmare for all who remained trapped within those haunted walls.

Will It Ever End

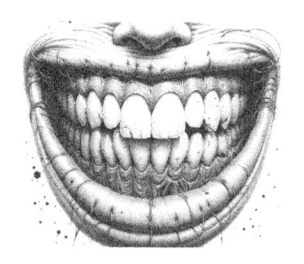

As we approached the threshold of the asylum, the first rays of dawn casting tentative light across our path, my father turned to look at me. His eyes once filled with warmth and intelligence, now echoed a hollow emptiness. "Son, let the doctor help you as he helped me," he murmured mechanically, his voice devoid of the emotions that had characterized our relationship. The words chilled me to the bone—a cruel echo of the warped mantra that had been repeated over the PA system. It was as if the doctor had left me with one final, haunting gift before our supposed escape.

This parting message was a striking reminder of the irreversible damage inflicted by the doctor's cruel experimentation. The lobotomy had ravaged his mind, erasing the man he once was and leaving behind a shell, a puppet repeating programmed lines. And my reflection—my face altered into a permanent, horrifying smile—mirrored the physical manifestation of the doctor's brutality. Together, we were the embodiment of his twisted capabilities, marked both inside and out.

The light of dawn, which should have been a symbol of hope and new beginnings, now felt mocking, highlighting our mutilations and the stark reality of our situation. As we stepped through the asylum's doors, the illusion of freedom shattered. The presence of staff and security, their faces a mix of shock and authority, signaled that our ordeal was far from over.

"Stop right there," commanded a security guard, stepping forward to block our path. The normalcy in his tone was surreal, jarring against the backdrop of our nightmarish experience.

"We just want to leave. We've been through enough," I pleaded, my voice cracking under the weight of desperation and exhaustion.

The guard's expression momentarily softened a flicker of sympathy passing over his features before professional detachment reclaimed his demeanor. "I'm sorry, but we have to take you both back inside. There are procedures we need to follow and paperwork to be signed. You can't leave just yet."

As we were gently but firmly led back into the asylum, the brief taste of freedom now cruelly withdrawn, the reality of our continued captivity settled heavily upon us. My father's repeated phrase, now a haunting refrain, played over in my mind, a reminder of the doctor's final, psychological violation.

As we were escorted back through the imposing corridors of the asylum, the irony of the situation wasn't lost on me. Here we were, my father and I, shambling figures of a nightmarish ordeal, being led not to freedom but to bureaucracy. A security guard, with a demeanor that seemed to blend kindness with an obligatory sternness, guided us into a small, nondescript room.

"Please, have a seat," he said, gesturing to a couple of uncomfortable-looking chairs. "We just need you to fill out some paperwork before you can leave."

The room, bare and fluorescently lit, contained a table strewn with forms and a couple of pens that looked as if they had seen better days. My father and I exchanged a look—a mix of disbelief and dark humor flickering between us. Here we were, part of a morbid 'family' outing that included surgical alterations and psychological terror, now being asked to sign non-disclosure forms as if we had just undergone a routine dental checkup.

As I picked up a pen, the absurdity of signing a nondisclosure agreement after such an ordeal almost made me laugh out loud. "They think a piece of paper is going to keep us quiet?" I whispered to my dad, who, despite his condition, managed a small, knowing smirk. It was a brief, shared moment of levity amid the darkness.

Before we could start scribbling our names, the door opened, and in walked the doctor, his presence as imposing as ever. But this time, he reached up and slowly pulled off his mask, revealing not the monstrous face I had imagined, but that of a benign, elderly man with kindly, twinkling eyes and a grandfatherly smile.

"Ah, I see you're getting acquainted with our paperwork," he chuckled, his voice warm and oddly comforting.

"I'm Dr. Blackwell. I apologize for the dramatics; occupational hazard, I'm afraid."

He moved to sit at the head of the table, his demeanor disarmingly gentle. "Now, I know this has all been rather strenuous, but we've administered the appropriate medication for your injuries, and I must insist you both come back for a checkup in about a week. Just to ensure everything is healing nicely, you understand."

It was surreal, watching this gentle old man discuss our 'treatment' as if we hadn't just been part of a twisted survival game. The disconnect between his grandfatherly appearance and the horrors he had orchestrated was jarring, yet his demeanor suggested this was just another day at the office for him.

My father, still a bit dazed, nodded slowly, his compliance a mixture of his lobotomy and the sedative effects of the medication. I, however, couldn't help but respond with a touch of sarcasm, the absurdity of the situation too potent to ignore.

"Sure, Dr. Blackwood, we'll just pencil that in right after our group therapy for traumatic experiences," I quipped, unable to resist the urge to underline the ludicrousness of his request.

Dr. Blackwell just smiled, apparently unbothered by my tone. "Excellent, my boy. Keeping a sense of humor is vital for recovery. We'll see you next week then."

As we signed the forms and were finally led out of the asylum—the real, unobstructed morning light greeting us—I couldn't shake the feeling of having just walked off the set of the strangest, most horrifying reality show ever conceived. And yet, the normalcy with which Dr. Blackwood and the staff treated the whole affair was perhaps the most unsettling part of all. It was a bizarre conclusion to weeks and weeks of terror, and as my father and I walked away, our steps lightened by the absurdity of it all, I knew this was a story that would need more than just medication and a follow-up appointment to process.

The week following our temporary release from River Road Asylum stretched out interminably, each day blending into the next with a monotonous grey haze that neither the sun nor the sporadic rains could dispel. My father, his mind shadowed and fractured from Dr. Blackwell's ruthless lobotomy, became my constant care. Watching over him, assisting with the simplest of tasks he once performed with thoughtless ease, was a stark and constant reminder of the horrors that awaited back at the asylum.

The house, once filled with the mundane sounds of daily life, now echoed with the unsettling quiet of convalescence. I administered medications that seemed to do little but keep him docile, changed bandages that covered wounds that were more mental than physical, and listened to the fragmented snippets of his thoughts, which surfaced between long stretches of vacant stares.

As the days passed, a strange anxiety began to take root within me. It was an unnerving blend of dread and an inexplicable pull towards the place of our torment. Each night, as I lay in bed, the shadows in my room morphed into the dark, elongated hallways of the asylum, and the distant sounds of the city mimicked the muffled cries of its inmates. Sleep became elusive, and when it did come, it brought little rest, filled instead with nightmares that replayed our ordeal in vivid, horrifying detail.

Dr. Blackwell's words, "See you soon, I'm sure," haunted me, echoing in my ears during quiet moments, reminding me of the impending return to his domain. My mind whirled with the possibility of what new cruelties awaited us, each thought more disturbing than the last.

By the time the day arrived for us to return to the asylum for our follow-up, the oppressive weight of inevitability had settled heavily on my shoulders. My father, largely oblivious to the significance of the day, required gentle coaxing to ready him for the trip. As I helped him into his coat, his vacant eyes met mine, offering no recognition, no comfort—only a hollow echo of the father he had once been.

The drive back to the asylum was cloaked in an oppressive silence. The building loomed in the distance, its stark, imposing structure growing ever larger as we approached. The sight of its familiar, foreboding walls sent a shiver down my spine. With each mile closer, my anxiety spiked; a visceral reaction to returning to the epicenter of our nightmare.

As we passed through the gates, the chilling familiarity of the grounds was overwhelming. The manicured lawns, so at odds with the despair housed behind those stone walls, were a cruel facade. My grip tightened on the steering wheel, knuckles whitening with the effort to maintain control—not just of the car, but of the fear gnawing at the edges of my resolve.

Stepping out of the car, I took a deep breath, trying to steel myself against the surge of emotions that threatened to overwhelm me. The air was crisp, the sky a too-bright blue above the dark silhouette of the asylum. It was a picture of eerie contrasts—much like the duality of our impending return: a blend of homecoming and a descent back into a waking nightmare. My father, docile and compliant, followed my lead as we walked back into the asylum, crossing the threshold into a reality where madness and medicine danced a macabre waltz. The doors closed behind us with a definitive thud, sealing our fate as we stepped deeper into Dr. Blackwell's twisted sanctuary.

The checkup unfolded under the sterile glare of the examination room lights, with Dr. Blackwell assuming the air of a benign, almost kindly physician. His demeanor was gentle, his movements precise as he examined the healing progress of the stitches that mapped my face and hands. Each touch was calculated, with an unsettling tenderness that belied the monstrous nature of his true intentions.

"Everything appears to be healing nicely," Dr. Blackwell commented, a smile playing at the corners of his mouth as he peered closely at my scars. "You're recovering well, which speaks volumes of your resilience, Ethan."

His words were soothing, almost caring, yet I found it difficult to reconcile this version of him with the orchestrator of the horrors we'd endured. As he continued his examination, the room filled with the quiet clinking of medical instruments, a soundtrack that seemed too normal given the context.

Seizing a moment of calm, I ventured to ask about Mike and Sarah. My voice was steady, but underneath, anxiety churned. "And how are Mike and Sarah doing?" I inquired, trying to keep my tone neutral.

Dr. Blackwell paused, setting down his tools and clasping his hands neatly in front of him. "Ah, Sarah," he began, his voice tinged with what appeared to be genuine satisfaction. "She's shown remarkable improvement. So much so, I believe she might be ready to leave us soon."

Relief washed over me at his words, a stark contrast to the dread that followed as he spoke of Mike. "As for Mike," he continued, his expression turning somber, "he has become quite indispensable to us here. I'm afraid he's found his calling, helping with various... projects. It's best for him to remain, where he can contribute and feel fulfilled."

The news hit like a gut punch. While Sarah's potential release was a sliver of hope, the idea of Mike remaining trapped within the asylum's walls, possibly forever, was a bitter pill to swallow.

With the checkup concluded, Dr. Blackwell offered a few parting words of encouragement that felt hollow, given the circumstances. We left the examination room with mixed emotions, the weight of Mike's fate heavy on my mind.

The short drive home was quiet, the car's engine humming softly as we navigated the roads leading away from the asylum. The distance did little to ease the tension, each mile home a reminder of the unresolved horrors left behind. As we drove, the scenery blurred past, a blunt nudge of the world moving on outside while parts of my life remained stagnant, locked within the confines of Dr. Blackwell's domain.

Arriving home, the familiarity of the surroundings offered little comfort. Stepping out of the car, the cool air felt refreshing, yet the sense of unease lingered, a silent specter of the ongoing ordeal. As I helped my father inside, the normalcy of opening our front door and stepping into the living room felt jarringly out of place, a mundane action at the end of an anything-but-normal day.

The house welcomed us back, but the shadows seemed deeper, each corner a reminder of the darkness we had momentarily escaped but not evaded. As I settled my father in, the promise to return for Mike and the hope for Sarah's release was the only beacons in the murky uncertainty that had become our lives.

One part of my mind screamed for escape, urging me to flee Talmage and never glance back. Yet, another part, inexplicably rooted in this haunted town, held me captive. There was a perverse allure in the horrors I had endured, a twisted fascination that gnawed at my sanity. It was as though I was caught in Dr. Blackwell's macabre spell, half-expecting, half-dreading that one day he might summon me again, inviting me back into his twisted games. This conflicting turmoil left me tethered to the place I most feared, trapped in a chilling cycle of fascination and horror.

Stepping back into the asylum was disconcerting, but encountering Dr. Blackwell around town was a surreal experience. Each encounter was a twisted reminder of our ordeal, as he greeted us with the same unsettling cheerfulness, behaving as if our past interactions had been nothing more than routine medical appointments. "Ah, my favorite patients! How are we feeling today?" he would chirp publicly, waving from across the street or approaching us in the local coffee shop as if we were old friends reconnecting. His demeanor was jovial and friendly, a stark contrast to the man who orchestrated nightmares behind closed doors. To the outside world, Dr. Blackwell was a pillar of the community, revered for his contributions to mental health and his supposed dedication to healing.

This bizarre public facade was compounded by interactions with others in town, like my friend Mike, who approached me one day while he was out walking with Dr. Blackwell as if the horrors of the asylum had never occurred. "Hey, how have you been? It's been too long!" Mike would say with a smile, clapping me on the back as if our last meeting had been at a mundane social gathering rather than as part of a sinister experiment. The normalcy with which he engaged with me, ignoring the dark undercurrents of our shared experiences, left me reeling, questioning the reality of our past interactions.

This veneer of normality made our experiences feel even more isolated and surreal. Walking through town, seeing Dr. Blackwell interact with unsuspecting locals, praising his work, thanking him for his service to the community—it all felt like a whimsical charade. Each friendly greeting from him, each casual conversation with Mike, was a mask that hid the chilling truth of his nature and the dark secrets of the asylum.

We were trapped not only by the memories of what we had endured but also by the outward normality of our tormentor's interactions with the world. Our lives had become a psychological cage, where the horrors we knew were hidden behind the friendly facade of a man who had mastered the art of public perception. In this twisted reality, laughter and light existed, but they were overshadowed by the knowledge of what lay beneath Dr. Blackwell's affable exterior. We lived with the constant reminder that beneath the surface of everyday normalcy, the darkness of the asylum lingered, ever-present and insidious.

A few weeks after our reluctant return to the asylum for the checkup, I noticed Sarah walking down the road past my house. The sight of her was jarring—she was clad in a faded hospital gown, her steps slow and aimless, her expression vacant. The morning sun did little to mask her pallor; she looked like a walking corpse, a chilling testament to the depth of Dr. Blackwell's experiments. The once vibrant and defiant friend I knew was now reduced to this ghostly figure, wandering seemingly without purpose or recognition of her surroundings.

I stepped out onto my porch, a sense of urgency mixed with dread tightening in my chest. "Sarah!" I called out, hoping to catch her attention, to break through whatever fog had enveloped her mind. But she didn't respond, didn't even pause or turn to acknowledge her name being called. Instead, she continued her slow, haunting march toward town, her figure growing smaller in the distance.

Frantic, I followed her, keeping my distance, not wanting to startle her. As we reached the town, people glanced her way, their expressions a mix of concern and curiosity, yet no one approached her. It was as if they sensed something deeply wrong, something unspoken that kept them at bay.

Sarah wandered through the streets, her presence casting a somber tone over the morning bustle. I tried several times to approach her, to get her to recognize me, to speak, anything that would show a sign of the Sarah I once knew. But each attempt was met with the same blank stare, the same unseeing eyes that looked through me as if I were a ghost.

Eventually, Sarah drifted further into town, blending into the crowd until I could no longer see her. I searched for hours, retracing our path, asking passersby if they had seen her, but it was as if she had vanished into thin air. No one had seen where she went or could recall more than a fleeting glimpse of her passing by.

As the day wore on, the realization that I had lost her, perhaps forever, settled heavily on me. The image of her hollow, unresponsive stroll haunted me. What had Dr. Blackwell done to her in the name of his twisted science? What horrors had she endured that left her in such a state?

The sorrow and frustration of being unable to help her weighed on me as I walked back home. The town, once familiar and comforting, now felt tainted, overshadowed by the dark influence of the asylum that loomed on its outskirts. The normalcy of daily life seemed a thin veneer over the chilling secrets that I knew lurked beneath.

Sarah's disappearance became another ghostly chapter in the story of Dr. Blackwell's asylum, a story marked by shadows and unanswered questions. Her walking corpse-like figure was etched into my memory, a haunting reminder of the cost of crossing paths with Dr. Blackwell. As I returned to the quiet of my home, I knew that the fight against his dark legacy was far from over, each victim's silence a call to action that I could not ignore.

No Escape

My days became a blur of restless nights and listless days. I wandered through town aimlessly, avoiding familiar faces who might ask questions I wasn't ready to answer. The local coffee shop, once a favorite place, now felt claustrophobic, filled with too many bright smiles and normal conversations that grated against my frayed nerves and ravaged face.

One particularly overcast afternoon, as I aimlessly walked past the asylum, I stopped and stared through the rot iron barrier. The building stood silent, a stark monument to suffering and secrets. My heart raced, and a cold sweat broke out across my forehead as I stared at the imposing structure. It was a physical manifestation of my turmoil, and in that moment, a reckless thought took hold—perhaps I should go back inside.

The idea was insane, yet it pulsed through me with an undeniable force. Maybe there were answers within those walls, maybe a confrontation with the site of my trauma would help exorcise the demons that seemed to grip my psyche. Or perhaps, I admitted to myself with a shiver, I was seeking the familiarity of pain, a known quantity in a world that now seemed unbearably alien.

Some friends from around town had recommended a psychiatrist, but I had always been reluctant to discuss my emotions. My father's staunch advice to suppress my feelings and "be a man" had deeply ingrained a philosophy of stoicism in me. This was the doctrine under which I had operated my entire life. However, lately, I felt as though my hold on reality was slipping through my fingers. The growing urgency to seek help gnawed at me. I knew that without intervention, I risked becoming a ghost of myself, aimlessly wandering the streets much like my dear friend Sarah, whose own battles had left her a mere shadow in the community. The thought of descending into that kind of existence spurred a quiet desperation in me, pushing me towards reconsidering the idea of therapy before I too, became a lost soul in our small town.

The entire town seemed shrouded in a conspiracy, their actions and words intricately woven into a sinister tapestry that I had yet to fully perceive. As I walked through its streets, the familiar smiles and nods of neighbors and shopkeepers masked a darker intent. Everyone, it seemed, played a part in a grand, orchestrated effort to draw me back to the asylum. Their motivations were hidden beneath layers of mundane interactions, they were puppets, or perhaps puppeteers, in a macabre play directed by unseen forces, possibly even Dr. Blackwell himself.

I finally broke down and began seeing a psychiatrist who was prescribed to me by Dr. Blackwell. During my sessions with the psychiatrist—a key actor in this clandestine drama—I found myself recounting the gruesome experiences within the asylum with a chilling level of detail and an unsettling fervor. "The scalpel felt almost natural in my hand," I told her, my voice steady, almost clinical, betraying a morbid fascination. "As I sliced through skin and sinew, I was both surgeon and butcher, peeling back the layers of human frailty to expose the quivering tissues beneath. The first incision was always the cleanest, a pristine breach in an otherwise unmarked canvas."

"The blood was perpetual," I continued, the words flowing with a grotesque enthusiasm. "It seeped from every cut, pooled in every cavity. It was an artist's red paint, vivid against the harsh white of bone and the visceral hues of internal organs. I remember how the blood's coppery scent filled the air, mingling with the sharp tang of antiseptic—the perfume of the operating theater."

"As I delved deeper into each body, searching for the severed pieces of myself—my fingers—it was like exploring a gnarled treasure map. Each organ I moved aside, each vessel I clamped shut, brought me closer to my goal. The resistance of tissue against my tools was both a challenge and a thrill. There was a power in reclaiming what had been taken from me, even if it was through such horrific means."

The psychiatrist listened, her expression unreadable behind a mask of professionalism, yet I could sense her interest, perhaps even approval, as I described my actions and the twisted satisfaction they brought me. "And how did it make you feel, wielding such control within that chaos?" she probed, her voice a soft coaxing to draw out more of my dark revelations.

"It was empowering," I admitted, a dark part of me resonating with the memory. "In a place where I was subjected to unimaginable horrors, taking an active role, even as grotesque as it was, made me feel like I was writing my script, altering my fate one cut at a time."

As I left her office, the realization that I was being manipulated to return to the asylum grew within me. Yet, the understanding of this manipulation was tangled with a perverse longing for the intensity and clarity that the horror had provided. The town, with its covert motivations and orchestrated normalcy, was a facade, and I was both a victim and a willing participant in its shadow play.

My recollection of the asylum's horrors, told with a sinister relish, haunted me—not just for the acts I had described but for the part of me that had thrived in that darkness. It was a chilling acknowledgment that the line between victim and perpetrator could blur, twisted by the psychological manipulations of those who pulled the strings of this never-ending dance. As the town conspired to send me back, part of me wondered if returning was inevitable, drawn by the dark allure of the horrors that awaited.

Returning home, the weight of my responsibilities and the chilling memories from the asylum pressed heavily on my mind. My father, once a strong and vibrant man, now sat silently in his chair by the window, a distant look in his eyes. The lobotomy performed by Dr. Blackwell had left him a casing of his former self, incapable of the simplest tasks without guidance. Caring for him was not just a physical challenge but an emotional battleground, watching the man who had raised me reduced to this state of vacant dependency.

Managing my creeping darkness was proving to be a daunting task. The whispers of the town, the manipulative encouragement to return to the asylum, and the vivid, gory memories that both horrified and invigorated me—everything was converging into a suffocating tapestry of despair and intrigue. I found myself barely functioning, caught in a cycle of sleepless nights filled with nightmarish recollections and days blurred by the monotony of care and the persistence of psychological turmoil.

It was during one particularly stark morning, as I watched my father muttering the same haunting refrain—"Son, let the doctor help you as he helped me"—that a desperate tenacity took hold. If there was any chance of reclaiming some semblance of our former lives, or at least of understanding the full extent of what had been done to us, it lay back at the source of our torment. I needed answers, and ironically, it seemed that only Dr. Blackwell could provide them.

With a heavy heart, I prepared for our return to the asylum. Packing a small bag with the essentials, I helped my father into the car, his movements sluggish and uncoordinated, his spirit as absent as his gaze. The three-minute drive back was quiet, the only sounds were the soft hum of the engine and the occasional murmur from my father, repeating that same chilling line that seemed to echo the town's unseen chorus.

As we pulled up to the pristine facade of the asylum, a sense of deja vu overwhelmed me, the immaculate exterior belying the horrors that lurked within. Dr. Blackwell was waiting for us at the entrance, his presence both menacing and oddly comforting in its familiarity. His smile was congenial, his hands open in greeting, yet his eyes held a depth of knowledge and calculation that made me feel at ease.

"Welcome back," he intoned, his voice smooth and reassuring. "I'm pleased you've decided to return. I believe we can offer the help you need." He said as if he knew the torment I had been going through.

Leading us back into the asylum, Dr. Blackwell guided us through the familiar corridors to his office, a room that felt more like a high-stakes psychological battleground than a medical professional's workspace. As my father sat quietly, lost in his broken world, Dr. Blackwell turned his full attention to me.

"Your struggles, both personal and as a caretaker, are exactly why I believe further treatment here could be beneficial," he explained, his voice soothing yet underlined with an authoritative edge. "We can explore more... innovative approaches to both your father's condition and you r afflictions."

The offer was tempting, a promise of relief wrapped in the guise of clinical care. Yet, the memories of my previous experiences here, the mutilations, and the manipulations held me back. As I sat across from Dr. Blackwell, the mastermind behind our suffering, I knew that any decision to engage further with his treatments bore risks that went beyond the physical. They threatened to ensnare us deeper in his psychological web, potentially stripping away what little autonomy we had managed to preserve.

Yet, here, perhaps, lay our only chance to find some answers or even a modicum of peace. With a deep breath, I nodded, agreeing to his terms, not out of trust but out of desperation, a gambit laid with the highest of stakes—our very minds and souls.

Returning Home

Dr. Blackwell's office, despite its association with past horrors, was somehow cozy and meticulously organized, a testament to the man's duality. As we settled into the deep, plush chairs, he busied himself with preparing tea, his movements deliberate and oddly nurturing. "It's important to make one's environment welcoming," he commented with a slight chuckle, "especially in our line of work." The kettle whistled softly in the background, adding a surreal layer of domesticity to the scene.

As he handed me a steaming cup, his demeanor shifted to one of earnest professionalism. "I understand these sessions can be quite stirring emotionally," he said, his tone laced with an empathetic tilt. "It's crucial to address both the mind and the heart."

Before I could sip the tea, the door opened, and in walked Mike, looking healthier and more vibrant than I remembered. The sight of him was a jolt—mixing relief and resentment. Memories of his abandonment clashed with the happiness of seeing an old friend. Mike greeted me with a broad, slightly nervous smile.

"Hey, it's really good to see you again," he said, his voice earnest, hinting at an undercurrent of past regrets.

Dr. Blackwell beamed at Mike, clearly proud. "Mike has made remarkable progress," he declared. "He's a testament to the transformative potential of our work here. I dare say, he's one of my most successful cases."

The pride in his voice was unmistakable as he turned to me. "Mike has truly seen the light, so to speak. It's amazing what the human mind can endure and adapt to."

He then leaned closer, his voice dropping to a conspiratorial whisper as if sharing a secret between old friends. "The experiments we conducted, the procedures Mike volunteered for—they were intense, yes, but also groundbreaking."

Mike nodded, a hint of pride mixed with something darker in his eyes. "It wasn't easy, but I learned a lot about myself. The things I've been through, the things I've done... it's all part of the journey."

Dr. Blackwell continued, his eyes gleaming with a mix of scientific fervor and a dash of madness. "Oh, the resilience we discovered! Blood transfusions from one patient to another to study immune responses, sensory deprivation to enhance other senses, psychological endurance tests that would redefine what you think is humanly possible."

As he described the gruesome details, a part of me felt a chilling fascination. The horror of what Mike had endured was undeniable, yet there was an allure to the knowledge and control Dr. Blackwell alluded to. The part of me that had thrived on the adrenaline and clarity of my darkest moments in the asylum felt a twisted kinship to Mike's experiences. I found myself envying his devotion and the attention he garnered from Dr. Blackwell.

"I almost want to be like Mike," I found myself thinking, the thought surprising even myself. There was something deeply unsettling yet magnetic about being so valued, so transformed by someone as brilliant yet twisted as Dr. Blackwell. The dichotomy of my emotions—repulsion, and intrigue—mirrored the complex interplay of terror and fascination that the asylum had always evoked in me.

Dr. Blackwell, observing my reaction, smiled knowingly. "It's a lot to take in, I know. But here, we're on the cutting edge—not just of science, but of discovering our true potential. Wouldn't you agree, Mike?"

Mike's affirmative nod seemed automatic, rehearsed, yet sincere. As the conversation continued, the boundaries of ethics and morality blurred into the background, overshadowed by the compelling allure of forbidden knowledge and the promise of becoming more than what I was—more like Mike, transformed and enlightened by the very horrors that haunted my memories.

Sitting in the cozy yet unnerving office of Dr. Blackwell, my emotions churned as I watched Mike's enthusiastic response to our discussions of the grueling experiments and transformations he had undergone. His zeal, contrasted with my internal turmoil, pushed me to broach a topic that had been pressing heavily on my mind—a topic filled with both hope and despair.

"Dr. Blackwell," I started, my voice hesitant, the weight of my father's condition like a stone in my chest, "is there... could we possibly do something for my dad? I mean, to fix what's been done to him?"

Dr. Blackwell's face took on a somber, yet strangely reassuring expression. He leaned forward, clasping his hands together as if weighing his next words very carefully. "Ethan, my dear boy," he began, his voice a soothing balm to my frayed nerves, "I understand your concern. It's quite touching, really. While the damage from the lobotomy is extensive, we are constantly making breakthroughs that were once thought impossible. I believe, with the right approach and... dedication, we might see some improvements."

His words, so full of promise and possibility, cut through the fog of my despair like a beacon. I felt a surge of irrational hope, a desperate grasp at the slim chance he presented. The logical part of my brain screamed warnings, but his magnetic influence, the authoritative assurance in his tone, overrode my better judgment. I believed him.

"However," Dr. Blackwell continued, his eyes glinting with a mix of anticipation and what could only be described as calculation, "before we attempt anything on your father, we need to ensure you're fully prepared for the complexities of such a procedure. This would require some practice, hands-on experience with other patients here."

Mike turned to me, his eyes alight with excitement, a distinct disparity to the chilling nature of what we were discussing. "Ethan, this is going to be so much fun," he said, his enthusiasm palpable. The sight of his eagerness, the readiness to dive back into the harrowing work that had so profoundly changed him, brought goosebumps to my skin.

Dr. Blackwell nodded approvingly at Mike's response, then turned his gaze back to me. "We have one final test for you both, to ensure you're ready. If you succeed, not only will you be more prepared to help your father, but you'll also have proven your commitment to the new frontiers we're exploring here."

The notion of 'testing' and 'preparation' by conducting surgeries and studies on other patients was horrifying, yet the part of me swayed by Dr. Blackwell's influence and the desperate need to help my father made me consider the proposal. The ethical lines blurred, overshadowed by the twisted justification that it could potentially lead to something beneficial.

"Will you join us, Ethan?" Dr. Blackwell asked, his voice both a challenge and a lure. "Are you ready to push the boundaries of what you believe is possible?"

Caught in the whirlwind of my emotions and the persuasive pull of Dr. Blackwell's charisma, I found myself nodding, agreeing to step further into the darkness that had already taken so much yet promised the possibility of redemption, however illusory it might be. As we left the office to begin our 'preparation,' the corridors of the asylum seemed less like halls of healing and more like passages to a new abyss that Mike and I were about to plunge into, together.

Mike and I exchanged nervous glances as we headed toward the operating room. The walk through the winding corridors of the asylum felt surreal, the echoing footsteps and the stark white walls closing in around us. The chilling instruction from Dr. Blackwell lingered in my mind, an ominous prelude to what awaited us. As I pushed open the heavy door to the operating room—a place of both fear and fascination that I knew all too well—a scene unfolded that I hadn't anticipated.

There, under the harsh, clinical lighting of the operating room, lay Dr. Blackwell himself, his body strapped securely to the table that had seen countless unspeakable procedures. The sight was disorienting, the master of horror now positioned as the subject. His eyes met mine as we entered, a strange gleam in them that was part excitement, part madness. "This is your final test," he announced, his voice eerily calm despite his vulnerable position. "You will be operating on me. I want the two of you to continue my work here. I'm growing old and need someone to take over for me."

Mike stepped forward, a hint of eagerness in his movements that brought with it a sense of unease. The room was filled with the usual array of surgical tools, each piece gleaming ominously under the bright lights. The air was thick with the antiseptic smell that I had come to associate with pain and fear, but now it was mixed with something else—a sense of power, a reversal of roles that was both terrifying and intoxicating.

"I've prepared everything you'll need," Dr. Blackwell continued, his voice steady as he gestured towards a tray of instruments with a slight nod of his head. "Don't worry, I've administered a local anesthetic to myself. I won't feel much, but I will be awake. I need to see your commitment, your precision."

As I approached the table, my hands trembled slightly, not just from the fear of what we were about to do, but also from the bizarre thrill that this twisted empowerment brought. Mike, already picking up a scalpel, seemed transformed, his usual hesitation replaced by a disturbing confidence. "Ethan, this is it," he whispered, almost reverently. "We're doing this. We're going to be part of something bigger."

I picked up another scalpel, the cold metal familiar and foreboding in my grip. Dr. Blackwell's eyes watched us both, a mentor evaluating his protégés. "Begin with an incision here," he instructed, his finger pointing to a marked area on his chest. "And remember, precision is key."

As the blade cut into his skin, the room was filled with the sound of Dr. Blackwell's calm breathing intermixed with the slight, wet noise of flesh being parted. Blood welled up at the incision site, dark and real against the stark whiteness of his skin. Each move we made was under his watchful gaze, his occasional nods of approval sending waves of both pride and horror through me.

The procedure was gruesome, a dance on the edge of ethical sanity, as we removed, examined, and then replaced each organ he directed us to explore. Dr. Blackwell's instructions were precise, and his fascination with our actions was both mentor-like and chillingly intense.

As the operation concluded, and we stitched the final sutures into his flesh, Dr. Blackwell let out a long, satisfied sigh. "Excellent," he murmured, a twisted smile playing on his lips. "You've both shown great potential. You are ready to continue my legacy."

Stepping back, I looked at Mike, then at Dr. Blackwell, the gravity of what we had just done—and what we were being invited to become—settling over me like a dark shroud. The asylum, once a place of horror, was now being offered as a kingdom, with us as its potential new rulers. The offer was monstrous, yet strangely fitting in the outrageous world Dr. Blackwell had created and we had now willingly stepped into.

My Fate Now Sealed

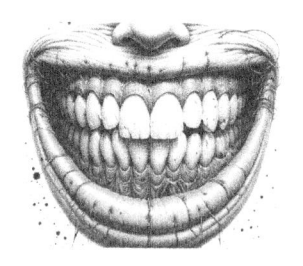

As we wiped the last traces of blood from the sutures sealing Dr. Blackwell's self-inflicted wounds, he beckoned us closer with a weak yet unmistakable authority. His face, though pale from the blood loss and strain, bore an expression of serene determination. "There is one more step you must undertake to truly understand the full scope of my legacy," he whispered, the tone both commanding and eerily calm.

"You are to perform a new type of lobotomy on me that Mike and I have been perfecting," Dr. Blackwell continued, his gaze piercing as it settled on me, then shifted to Mike. "This will be your ultimate test, to not only execute the procedure but to also decide my fate, to place me among my patients, where I will finally be free of the burdens of my consciousness."

The gravity of his request settled heavily in the sterile air of the operating room, charged with a strange anticipation. Mike and I exchanged a glance, a silent communication filled with both horror and a peculiar curiosity that had been cultivated by our experiences in the asylum.

Dr. Blackwell, sensing our hesitation, gave a nod toward a tray that had been meticulously prepared with various surgical tools. "You will find everything you need here," he instructed. "I will guide you through the process. Do not hesitate; this is the path to truly grasping the depths of the human mind."

Reluctantly, I stepped forward and selected a small, gleaming instrument designed for cranial penetration. Mike assisted, his hands steadier than I had ever seen them, as we positioned Dr. Blackwell's head to expose the precise area of his skull for the operation.

"Make an incision here," Dr. Blackwell directed, his finger tracing a line on his temple, remarkably composed as he dictated his dissection. "Then, you will need to drill a small hole through the skull. Be precise. You are not merely altering the physical state, but freeing the psyche from its corporeal bonds."

As I cut into the flesh of his temple, the skin parted under the blade with a faint, wet sound, a disgusting reminder of the reality of our actions. Blood trickled down the side of his face, pooling into the crevices of the operating table. Mike handed me the drill, his eyes wide with a mix of fear and fascination. I positioned it against the thin, marked spot on Dr. Blackwell's skull and began to bore into the bone. The drill whirred, a high-pitched grinding noise that echoed revoltingly in the small room.

"Deeper, just a bit more," Dr. Blackwell coached, his voice unnervingly steady. "Now, stop. That's enough.

Now, for the Leucotome." He directed us to a slender, pointed tool designed specifically for lobotomies. As I inserted the Leucotome through the hole in his skull, his eyes fluttered slightly, but his voice did not waver. "Insert it carefully. Rotate slightly... there, you've reached the frontal lobes. Now, sever the connections. Swiftly."

I manipulated the tool as instructed, feeling a resistance that gave way with a sickening ease. The deed was done. We had severed the very essence of Dr. Blackwell's cognitive abilities.

"Now, stitch the incision," he murmured, his voice growing fainter. "Place me among my creations, my patients. Let me be... free."

As Mike and I complied, stitching the wound with hands that trembled with the enormity of our actions, we were silent. Once completed, we transported Dr. Blackwell, now barely conscious, to one of the patient rooms, laying him gently among those he had once treated—and tormented.

Stepping back into the empty corridor of the asylum, the weight of what we had become hung between us. We had crossed a threshold beyond which there was no return, fully entwined now in the legacy of Dr. Blackwell. As we left his motionless form among his patients, his final wish granted, a chilling realization settled over us: the asylum was ours to command, a realm of shadows we now ruled with a dark and burdened sovereignty.

The doors of the asylum closed behind us with a resonant thud, sealing away the outside world and cocooning us in our new realm. As Mike and I walked down the dimly lit corridor, the air was thick with the aftermath of what we had done. Dr. Blackwell was now just another patient, his mind as fragmented and lost as those he had once experimented upon. His final instructions echoed in our minds; a sinister legacy passed down through the very act that had supposed to free him.

In the days that followed, the asylum took on a new rhythm, dictated by our hands. We were its masters now, the keepers of secrets and practitioners of dark arts disguised as treatments. Our rule was unchallenged, our authority absolute, fed by the whispers of madness and the cries of the hidden.

We had brought our friend, Sarah, back, once vibrant and fierce, roamed the halls like a ghost. Her presence was a constant reminder of our descent from victims to perpetrators. She rarely spoke, and when she did, her words were cryptic, disjointed—yet they carried the weight of unspeakable knowledge. Her transformation was perhaps the most tragic, a vivid illustration of the cost of our new-found power.

My father, too, was changed. Where once there had been the repetitive drone of his conditioned phrases, there was now only silence. He wandered the gardens of the asylum, a figure lost in time, his eyes empty but occasionally flickering with faint, unspoken recognition of the horrors that surrounded him. I watched over him, a protectorate role that felt more like a penance.

Mike embraced his role with an unsettling zeal. He delved deeper into the experimental therapies we had inherited, pushing boundaries with a reckless abandon that often left me cold. Yet, I could not deny the allure of the control it granted us, the godlike power to alter reality within the walls of our domain.

As the new rulers of the asylum, our days were filled with dark decisions and grimier deeds. The outside world seemed a distant memory, a faint echo of normalcy that no longer held any appeal. We were entities of the asylum now, shaped and molded by its legacy of despair and dominion.

One evening, as a storm raged outside, its fury mirroring the chaos of our existence, a gathering took place in the main hall. The patients, Mike, Sarah, my father, and I—all of us were there, a twisted family united under the banner of madness. Lightning illuminated our faces, revealing the scars, both physical and psychological, that we bore.

Dr. Blackwell, his mind now as fragmented as his victims, watched from his wheelchair, a smile playing upon his lips—a smile that chilled me to the bone. It was then I realized the full extent of our damnation. In our quest for control and understanding, we had become the embodiment of the asylum's darkest impulses.

The realization hit me with the force of the thunder that shook the building. We were not just running the asylum; we were its truest patients, caught in an endless cycle of horror that we perpetuated. Our reign was not one of power but of profound and pervasive madness.

In that climactic moment, as the storm reached its peak, I understood that the asylum would forever hold us in its grip, a grip as unyielding as the madness that pulsed through its veins. Sarah, her eyes meeting mine across the crowded room, finally spoke, her voice clear amidst the chaos: "We are the asylum," she said, a statement of terrifying acceptance.

And so, our fates were sealed, intertwined with the legacy of the place that had shaped us. We were the rulers of a kingdom of madness, destined to dwell in the shadows we had once feared, now the architects of the darkness that enveloped us. The asylum was our domain, our curse, and our sanctuary—forever.

Join my newsletter

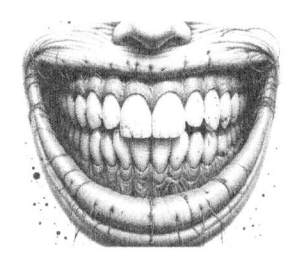

For new content and free short stories click the link below to join my newsletter. Be the first to know about exciting new book news and subscriber-only content.

https://dl.bookfunnel.com/5u57nso4xv

Printed in Great Britain
by Amazon